Did I dare tell?

Dear **D**iary:

Proud. There was that word again. Why would anyone be proud of the world's biggest phoney? I don't remember how I got out of the classroom, except I remember clutching Nancy's arm very tightly.

"Lizzie, are you sure you're okay? You really do look a little strange."

I hesitated. Nancy was my friend, the one person I could really trust. Did I dare tell her the terrible thing I had done? No, I needed to be alone to think things over. I was in the biggest mess of my whole life and I had no idea what to do next.

THE LIE

Carrie Randall

AN
APPLE
PAPERBACK

SCHOLASTIC INC.
New York Toronto London Auckland Sydney

ISBN 0-590-44024-1

Copyright © 1991 by Mary Lou Kennedy. All rights reserved. Published by Scholastic Inc. APPLE PAPERBACKS is a registered trademark of Scholastic Inc.

12 11 10 9 8 7 6 5 4 3 2 1   1 2 3 4 5 6/9

Printed in the U.S.A.   40
First Scholastic printing, May 1991

KEEP OUT!!

(This means you!)

This diary is the property
of

Elizabeth
Jane
Miletti

ALL TRESPASSERS WILL BE
PROSECUTED!

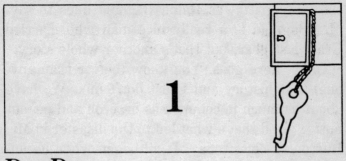

1

Dear **D**iary:

This has been one of the worst days of my entire life! On a scale of one to ten, it was a minus twenty-three. I, Lizzie Miletti, made a total jerk out of myself in front of my sixth-grade history class. When I tell you the gory details, you'll see why I am soooo embarrassed.

But maybe I'd better start at the beginning. I'm glad I don't have any secrets from you, Diary. I've been writing in you for such a long time that you know everything about me. Especially all the really important things. You know I'm eleven years old, and that I'm the middle kid in my family. I have two older brothers: Josh, sixteen; Adam, thirteen; and two younger sisters: Darcy, eight; and Rose, four. And of course you know that my mom used to be a nurse and that my dad works for Roth Frozen Food Company. What else? Well, you know that my best friend is Nancy Underpeace, and that my grandmother, Gram, is probably the most important person in my life.

1

That probably covers the big stuff. But down to the nitty-gritty, as Ralph Bagnold likes to say. Mr. Bagnold is a really nice man who married Gram last year, but that's another whole story.

Okay, here goes. You know (better than anyone) that history and I just don't mix. We have about as much in common as broccoli and peanut butter. And that's what led to the disaster in Mr. Burrows's class today. It all began when he unfolded a gigantic chart covered with names and dates. Everyone groaned. Everyone except my friend Nancy, who is a history nut. She gobbles up facts and figures like Pac Man eats dots. Nancy is dyslexic and has a little trouble reading, but she's a whiz at memorizing. She thinks history is fun, but I don't agree. Who wants to read about dead people?

But back to the classroom. I looked at the map, yawned a couple of times, and sneaked a look at the clock. Thirty-five minutes till lunch. Question: How was I going to stay awake? (Answer: I didn't).

I tried to put my best "interested look" on my face, but I felt like my eyelids were Velcroed together. One minute Mr. Burrows was talking about the Indian Wars, and the next minute I was paddling downstream in a buffalo-skin canoe. I was navigating a tricky bend in the river when it happened.

"Miss Miletti? Miss Miletti!"

My heart flip-flopped and my body lurched forward like a dummy in a seat belt ad. But that wasn't the worst part. I woke up and made this awful snorting noise!

"Aaaargh!" I blinked and found that everyone in my sixth-grade class at Claremont Elementary was staring at me. And not only staring but giggling like crazy. It sounded like a laugh track for the world's funniest TV show. Samantha Howard was chuckling nonstop, like a kitten with hiccups. (Samantha, blonde and beautiful, is *not* my favorite person, and I am not hers.) Donald Harrington, the class jerk, hee-hawed like a donkey, and even Billy Watts cracked up. He clapped his hand over his mouth, pretending to have a coughing fit, but I knew better. Billy Watts is the only boy in our class who seems human, and I'm sure he felt sorry for me. But he couldn't feel as sorry for me as I did for myself. I decided that my life was ruined!

Nancy, as usual, tried to cheer me up as we walked home together. "It's not the end of the world, you know," she said, skipping to avoid a puddle. "Lots of kids fall asleep in class."

"They do?"

"Well, maybe not lots, but it happens."

I groaned, remembering the look on Mr. Burrows's face. He looked annoyed and disappointed, as if I had let him down.

"You know what I think?" Nancy went on. "If

you do a super job on this term paper, he'll probably forget all about it."

The term paper! I glanced at her, my heart sinking another notch. I had been trying to block the assignment out of my mind. "You had to remind me," I said, only half teasing. The term paper was due in six weeks and counted for one third of our grade.

"It'll be fun," she said cheerfully. "I'm going to get started early, aren't you?"

"Um, I hadn't really thought about it," I mumbled, turning up the collar of my denim jacket against the rain. I glanced over at Nancy, who was wearing a yellow slicker that was at least three years old. To say that Nancy isn't interested in clothes is an understatement. In some ways, she just refuses to grow up. Her favorite outfit is an old Smurfs sweatshirt and a pair of jeans that look like she's been climbing trees in them. She actually carried a Snoopy lunchbox to school until the handle broke last year.

Nancy and I are opposites in a lot of ways. She's the tallest girl in the class, and has thick, straight blonde hair. I'm petite with short, frizzy dark hair. We've known each other since we were born, and we do have one thing in common — we both hate our names! Nancy hates her last name, Underpeace, because the kids call her everything from Underpants to Undertaker. I hate my first name,

4

Lizzie. It's short for Elizabeth, but I wish people would call me Beth, or Liza. Lizzie sounds like a kid's name, but I guess I'm stuck with it.

Mom and Rose were in the kitchen when we walked in, and a big pot was bubbling on the stove. "You're just in time for a taste test," Mom said, smiling at Nancy and me. My father is always trying out his strange new products on us.

"Oh no," I said, tossing my books on the table. "I've had enough disasters for one day."

"C'mon, where's your spirit of adventure?" Mom spooned a slimy green concoction into Rose's dish. "I bet Rose will like it."

That didn't prove anything and Mom knew it. Rose, who is only four years old, is a Human Garbage Disposal.

"It smells very interesting, Mrs. Miletti," Nancy said politely. She looked at Rose's dish and nearly gagged. "What — what is it?"

Mom brushed a stray lock of hair out of her eyes and took a casserole dish out of the oven. "It's part of a new advertising campaign," she said. "The wonderful world of pasta. Rose is trying the Macaroni Supremo." I noticed that even Rose was struggling. She thoughtfully licked the spoon and then wrinkled her nose. If you can picture macaroni covered with thick green pea soup, you get the idea.

5

"There's some dessert pasta in the microwave," Mom said bravely.

"Pasta for dessert?" I wasn't even sure I wanted to know about it.

"It's very experimental. Chocolate-covered spaghetti. They think it will start a new trend." Even Mom looked a little doubtful at that one.

"We'll have to pass, Mom," I said, heading for the stairs. I patted my notebook. "Big term paper coming up."

As soon as we escaped to my room, I flopped on the bed. "That was a narrow escape," I said, giggling. "Maybe I'll come to your house for dinner tonight."

"We're having leftovers," Nancy said, curling up on the window seat. "Mom says she just doesn't feel like cooking for two people." Nancy looked a little sad, and I knew she was thinking about her parents' divorce. Her father moved to Detroit and even though she sees him every other weekend, it just isn't the same.

"Do you want to play some records?" I asked, hoping to cheer her up.

"I thought we were going to start working on our history papers." She looked surprised.

"Gosh, I just said that for Mom's benefit." I rolled over and looked at her. "Besides, it's not due for months."

"Weeks."

I shrugged. "Whatever."

Nancy reached for a throw pillow and hugged it to her chest. "You know, there are so many great topics, I don't know where to start."

Darn, I thought. I could *not* get her mind off that stupid term paper. "Uh-huh." I thought Nancy would pick up on how bored I was, but no such luck.

"Just think of it," she said brightly. "We can pick anything that happened in American history, all the way from Colonial days to World War II."

"Amazing."

She sat bolt upright, her eyes flashing. "Maybe I'll do my paper on George Washington." She paused. "Did you know he had wooden teeth?"

"No, I only knew he was the father of our country."

"It's those little things that make history come alive," Nancy said.

I didn't bother stifling a giant yawn. As far as I was concerned, a bolt of lightning couldn't make history come alive. I tuned out the rest of what Nancy was saying and mentally redecorated my room.

At the moment, my room has powder blue walls, and a patchwork quilt on the bed. Every time I've tried to change it, it's ended up as a disaster.

"So what do you think?" Nancy said, jolting me

back to the present. "Should I stick with Washington, or go for the Industrial Revolution?"

"Mmm," I said, pretending to ponder. I turned my Empire State Building snowball paperweight upside down and watched all the snowflakes flutter skyward and then settle on the bottom. "I think you should stick with Washington," I said finally.

Nancy nodded. "I think you're right." She stood up and shrugged into her slicker. "In that case," she said generously, "you can do your paper on the Industrial Revolution."

"Oh, thanks."

"That's okay," she said very seriously. She hadn't noticed that I was rolling my eyes. "After all, what are friends for?"

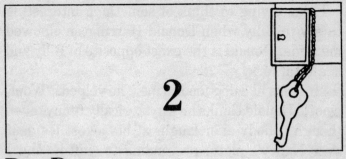

2

Dear **D**iary:

I was amazed when Nancy bought the lunch special today and told her so.

"I can't believe it," I said, peering at her plate as we headed for a table in the Claremont cafeteria. "Why would anybody buy something with a name like 'Beefy Biscuit'?"

"I just wasn't thinking," Nancy admitted. "I meant to buy the macaroni and cheese, but somehow I ended up with this awful *glop*." She looked down and winced. "I wonder what it *really* is?"

"Maybe it's a mutation," a voice from behind us said. "Nobody knows where it comes from! Nothing can stop it! It's the Glop from Outer Space. Coming soon to a theater near you."

Nancy giggled and I turned to smile at Billy Watts, the cutest boy in sixth grade. And also the nicest. I should know, because one time I danced three whole dances with him in the school gymnasium. (Which absolutely *killed* Samantha Howard, who didn't get to dance at all.)

I was trying to think of something interesting to say to Billy when Donald Harrington elbowed me aside. Donald is the exact opposite of Billy and is a total jerk.

"It looks like dog food to me," he yelped. "Woof, woof!" Donald thinks he's hysterically funny, even though nobody ever laughs at his jokes. He bent over Nancy's plate, pretending to sniff it, and I was tempted to push his face into it.

"Look, there's a table over there," I said, grabbing Nancy so we could make our getaway.

"I'm seeing my father this weekend," Nancy said, pushing her canned peas into a neat pile. "We're going on a walking tour of historic buildings on Saturday, and on Sunday we're going to brunch at a fancy hotel."

"I'm spending Saturday with Gram and Ralph," I said, munching on a big juicy apple. Somehow the cafeteria hasn't figured out a way to ruin apples but I'm sure they're working on it. "We're going to spend the morning making cookies for a party Gram's giving, and then Ralph is taking us to a country inn for lunch."

"A country inn?" Nancy looked impressed. "Your grandmother always does such cool things. You're really lucky, you know?"

"I know." Gram is the bright spot in my life. I'm lucky to have a great mom and dad, and four brothers and sisters, but there's nobody in the world like Gram. She always understands me, and I can always go to her for help and advice. She's more than a grandmother; she's like a special friend.

Nancy likes her, too. She thinks it's great that I have a grandmother who acts so young. Gram sells real estate and is such a good swimmer that she can do underwater somersaults.

I was just about to tell Nancy a funny story about the day Gram and I went shopping when Samantha Howard plunked her tray down on our table.

"I guess we'll have to sit here," she said in a disgusted voice. "It's the only place that has three seats together."

Samantha was with her two snooty friends, Candace Quinn and Jessica Aldridge. They always remind me of the two nasty stepsisters in *Cinderella*, because they never miss a chance to put someone down. Usually Nancy and me.

"I guess so," Candace said doubtfully. She edged her tray as far away from mine as possible. Both Candace and Jessica admire Samantha (why, I don't know) and try to be just like her. They think she's incredibly cool, and whenever Samantha wears something new, they turn up in the same thing a week or two later.

Samantha glanced at Nancy's beat-up sweatshirt and wrinkled jeans. "Nice outfit," she purred in her silky voice. "Did you just come from gym?"

Candace and Jessica giggled on cue, and Samantha looked very pleased with herself. I felt sorry for Nancy, whose cheeks were flaming, but I wished that she would wear decent clothes for once! I've never met anyone with less interest in fashion, and she could look really great if she wanted to. But Nancy dresses like a little kid who likes to make mud pies in the backyard.

"It's one of my father's college sweatshirts," Nancy said quietly. "I happen to like it!"

"Don't bother explaining," I told her. I nodded toward Samantha who was tossing her long blonde hair over her shoulder like someone in a shampoo commercial. Every hair on her head was perfect and her nails were painted the same shade of pink as her ten-button top.

"I think I may pick another topic for my term paper," Nancy said after a couple of minutes. I noticed she had completely given up on her sliced water buffalo-on-toast and was tackling the Jell-O.

"Really? I thought you had decided on George Washington and his wooden teeth."

"I don't know. I just think it would be more fun to pick a famous woman in American history and write about her."

"You mean like Betsy Ross or Harriet Tubman?"

She looked surprised. "I hadn't thought about

them, but that's a good idea. How about you? Have you made up your mind?"

I scrunched up my face like I was thinking hard. "I'm still working on it."

"Don't wait too long," she warned me. "Remember, the sooner you pick a topic, the sooner you can get started."

"Hmm, I'll remember that," I said, wishing I could change the subject. Luckily, Nancy and I could talk about anything we wanted because Samantha and her friends weren't even listening to us.

"What do you think of Robert Wilkins?" I heard Samantha say to Candace in a low voice.

"He's *really* smart," Candace whispered back. "I've heard he does algebra equations for *fun*."

"You're kidding!" Jessica piped up. I should have mentioned that Samantha and her friends just pick at their food, and spend the whole time checking out the cute guys in the cafeteria.

"I know he's *smart*," Samantha snapped, picking up the conversation, "but do you think he's cute?"

Jessica laughed. "Not as cute as Billy Watts." She paused and gave a sly smile. "But you already know that."

I sneaked a look at Samantha and her blue eyes were icy. For some reason (which is a total mystery to her) Billy Watts has zero interest in her. She has *never* forgiven me for dancing with him in the gym, and I guess she figures her reputation as "queen of the sixth grade" has slipped a notch.

And there's another reason she can't stand me. She has a crush on my brother Adam, but as far as he's concerned, she's invisible!

"Do you want to go to the library after school today?" Nancy said, breaking into my thoughts.

"The library?" I was watching Donald Harrington stick two straws up his nose for his rhino imitation. He does this at least once every lunch period, even though it grosses everyone out.

"To work on our term papers," Nancy said. "I won't be able to get any work done over the weekend because I'll be in Detroit. And you'll be busy with Gram and Ralph," she said pointedly.

"Oh yeah. I guess you're right." I tried to put a little enthusiasm in my voice, but Nancy wasn't fooled.

"We'll search the card catalogue for reference books, and then we'll try the magazine index, too."

"Sounds good." I was already tuning out, watching Billy Watts. He has a really nice smile and I like the way his eyes crinkle when he laughs.

"Honestly, Lizzie, you're a million miles away!" She was already picking up her tray and pushing back her chair.

"Not really," I said, scrambling to keep up with her. It was the truth. I wasn't a *million* miles away. Just four tables!

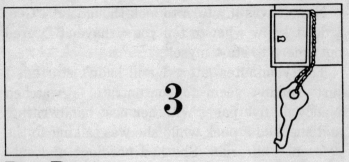

3

Dear **D**iary:

Usually I like going to the library, but yester-
day afternoon my heart just wasn't in it. Nancy
was organized as usual, which shouldn't surprise
me because that's the way she is about everything. She came armed with dozens of index cards
and Magic Markers.

"I brought enough supplies for both of us," she
said brightly. I tried to stifle a huge yawn, but
she was too quick for me.

"That's great," I said, trying to sound interested. "I guess we can really get started now."

"We sure can." She flipped open a looseleaf
notebook on the long oak table and looked
thoughtful. "Have you settled on a topic yet?"

"Um, not really," I hedged. "There are so many
possibilities."

"Exactly! But that's what makes research so
much fun. I think I've narrowed it down to Betsy
Ross or George Washington, but I'm still open for
ideas."

15

Now it was my turn to look thoughtful. "Gee, I don't know what to tell you. I haven't figured out where to start myself. . . ."

Thirty minutes later, I still hadn't started. I just couldn't seem to concentrate! I watched Nancy fill five pages with her neat handwriting, and sneaked a peek while she was talking to the reference librarian. She had headings and sub-headings, and everything color coded. I was really impressed.

"What do you think?" She had come up behind me quietly, and I nearly jumped out of my skin.

"I think it's great," I said, covering my own scratch pad with my hand. It was covered with doodles and squiggly initials. Last year, someone gave me a calligraphy set for Christmas. I've never really learned how to do all the fancy lettering, but I've had a lot of fun trying.

Nancy sat down and didn't say anything for a minute. We know each other so well, we can practically read each other's minds, and she knew what was going on. "You know, Lizzie," she said gently, "if you're stumped for ideas, I can give you a little hint. Do what I do."

"What's that?"

"Just prowl around the library, and keep an open mind. You'd be surprised how ideas just hit you in here. You can be wandering through the stacks or looking through the card catalogue, and suddenly a great topic will jump right out at you."

"Good idea!" I said, getting up. I seriously doubted that a great topic was waiting for me — anywhere! — but I was dying to get up and move around.

I knew exactly where I wanted to go first. The magazine racks! I grabbed the latest issue of *Teen Star*. It was a special issue on how to be popular, and I couldn't wait to read it.

I settled down with an article on how to talk to boys. I figured that was probably my weakest area, because sometimes I get tongue-tied when I'm around them. Especially really cute boys like Billy Watts. Nancy says I'm making too big a deal of it, but I notice she's not so great in that department herself. I think we both have a lot to learn.

I curled up in a spongy leather chair next to the window and started to read. After a few minutes, I realized that I had been on the wrong track all along. According to "Tina," who was starring in her very own television show, talking to boys was a snap. She had loads of good advice, but I could see that learning to talk to boys was going to take up a lot of my time. It was almost as much trouble as a term paper! And it even required research . . .

"How are you doing?"

It was Nancy! "Uh fine, just fine." I tucked *Teen*

Star under my notebook and scrambled to my feet. Nancy was looking at me very suspiciously, and I'm sure she knew I hadn't been working at all.

"So, what's your topic?"

I shrugged. "Still looking. How are you doing?" I tried to smile and look relaxed. That was another little hint from Tina. She said you should never *look* nervous, even if you are.

"I'm on my way to the stacks," she said happily. "I think I've narrowed it down, but there are a few more things I want to check."

"Don't let me keep you," I said, willing her to walk away. I wanted to finish reading Tina's tips before I put the magazine back.

"If you need any help — " she began, but I cut her off with a friendly shove.

"Go!" I said playfully. "I'll catch up with you later."

I waited until she was out of sight, and slumped back in the chair. I skimmed the rest of the article, which wasn't as helpful as I had hoped. Tina said that to be a good conversationalist, you had to be an interesting person. I thought about that for a minute, and decided to ask Gram about it. How did you know if you were interesting or not?

I made sure Nancy was nowhere in sight, and quietly replaced the magazine. I bent down to the bottom shelf and on the way up, I nearly bumped heads with an incredibly cute boy!

"Sorry," I muttered, just as he said the same thing. He had sandy hair, warm brown eyes, and kind of a shy smile. He wasn't as cute as Billy Watts, but he was definitely in the running. I struggled to think of something to say and as usual my mind was a blank. And then it hit me. All I had to do was ask him a question about *anything*. He was already turning away, so I knew I had to act fast.

"Excuse me," I blurted out, "but are you finished with that magazine?"

He looked surprised and glanced at the magazine in his hand. "Sure," he said, passing it to me. "But this is last month's issue. The new one hasn't come out yet."

Tina was right. This was a cinch! "That's okay. I just wanted to take a quick look at it." I looked down. It was a copy of *Geology Unlimited*. Bingo! He was into rock collecting! This was something I know a *lot* about, because Adam has a rock collection.

"Wow, that's a fantastic piece of quartz on the cover!" I waited for his reaction, and I felt encouraged when he stopped in his tracks.

"It's a great specimen," he said slowly. "But you should see the samples of zircon inside, they're really out of sight." He flipped through the pages until he found one. We were standing side by side, and for once in my life I didn't feel the least bit nervous or tongue-tied. Tina's advice was working like a charm! He moved a little closer (or maybe I imagined it!) and the next thing you know we were talking a mile a minute. He seemed surprised that I knew all about rocks and crystals, and told me about his collection.

We could have talked about rocks *forever*, but we were interrupted by a girl with long red hair who could have stepped off the cover of *Teen Star*.

"Oh here you are!" she said, putting an arm around his shoulder. She was tall and thin and wore a great-looking white jumpsuit. "I'm starving. Can we get something to eat?"

"Sure." He paused and looked at me. "We were just talking about rock formations."

The girl's eyes flickered over me without any interest. "Gosh, I bet he drove you crazy going on and on about those stupid rocks."

"No, really, I love rocks — " I started to say, but it was too late.

"Honestly, Steve, how can you be interested in that . . . *gravel*? It looks like it belongs in somebody's driveway." She stopped talking long enough to fling her other arm around him. "Now can we please get out of here before I faint from hunger?"

He laughed good-naturedly and gave her a little hug. "Right away." They started to move down the aisle, and he looked over his shoulder at me.

"It was nice to talk to you." Very polite. Very disinterested.

"Yeah, sure," I said, trying to sound casual. I was beginning to wonder if Tina knew what she was talking about after all!

I was walking idly by the reference desk when Nancy caught up with me. "What a day this has been!" Her eyes were shining and she looked very pleased with herself. "I finally narrowed down my topic, I've started my research, and I think I even have a first sentence." She was ticking the items off on her fingers.

"I'm impressed." I couldn't resist teasing her just a little, but she missed it.

"The reference librarians are really great," she added. "You can ask them anything, and if they don't know the answer, they can look it up. One of them even called the Library of Congress for me. Can you imagine that?"

I shook my head. I was still thinking about Tina and how she would have handled the girl in the white jumpsuit.

"Lizzie, you're not listening."

"I am too." I tried to look a little indignant, so she would believe me. I looked outside, and was surprised to find that it was getting dark. "Gosh, I guess we better get going," I said, just as the librarian announced that they were closing.

"Yeah, let's step on it. I've got to get home on

time because I'm fixing dinner for Mom and me tonight."

"Spaghetti?"

Nancy laughed. Spaghetti is her favorite food and she fixes it whenever it's her turn to cook. "What else?" She shrugged into her jacket and picked up a giant pile of books. "Well, at least we got a lot done on our papers today," she said. "You know what Mr. Burrows says. The first step is always the hardest."

"Oh yeah, I know what you mean." I shuffled some papers around and closed my notebook. The first step? I hadn't moved an inch! At the rate I was going, I'd be a hundred and two and still working on my stupid paper!

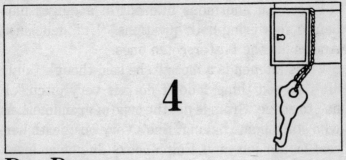

4

Dear **D**iary:

I really love Saturdays. The first part of the day is never too thrilling, because we all pitch in to clean up the house. Nobody gets excused, not even Rose, who picks up her toys and makes a stab at cleaning up the playroom. You can't expect a four-year-old to get too excited over cleaning up, but if you make a game out of it, Rose always falls for it.

Gram was in the kitchen when I dashed over to her house at ten-thirty. "Perfect timing," she said. She wiped her floury hands on her apron and hugged me. "I just took a tray of gingersnaps out of the oven. Ralph's out doing some errands, so you're the first one to try them."

"I thought you were going to wait for me to help you."

"Don't worry. There's plenty left to do. I need two more batches of chocolate chip, and a pan of brownies. How are the cookies? And should the brownies be chocolate or butterscotch?"

I took an enormous bite out of a gingersnap before answering both questions. "Um, delicious. And make the butterscotch ones."

"This kitchen is a mess," she said thoughtfully. "It's a good thing I don't do this very often." I had to agree. Gram is *not* the type of grandmother who stays home baking. She's very busy with her real estate job, and Ralph cooks dinner at least half the time.

"What's the occasion, anyway?"

Gram lifted another tray out of the oven and set it gingerly on the counter. "I'm having a surprise party for my students. They've been so much fun that I want to do something special for them." Once a week, Gram volunteers to teach English as a second language to foreigners. All the students are adults, and they're really eager to learn. Sometimes Gram even asks me for some examples of slang expressions to teach them.

"Gram, can I ask you something?"

"Of course." She rubbed her nose, and left a trail of white flour. "Did I just put two eggs in here?"

"And half a cup of sugar."

She laughed. "Good. For a minute there, I thought I was really losing it. Now, what did you want to know?"

I hesitated. How could I be sure Gram would tell me the truth? After all, she was my grandmother. I decided to go for it. "Gram, don't laugh, but I have to ask you something and I want you to give me a straight answer."

"Shoot."

"Am I an interesting person?"

Gram didn't laugh. Instead, she took off her reading glasses and peered at me thoughtfully. "Why yes, Lizzie. I would say you were a very interesting person." She must have known what was going through my mind because she added, "And I'm not just saying that because I love you. You're warm, and humorous, and a lot of fun to be around."

I didn't say anything for a minute. Gram's opinion meant a lot to me.

"What brought this up?" she said, puzzled.

"Just something I was reading in a magazine." I told her about the *Teen Star* article, and about Tina's tips.

"You don't need tips to be interesting, Lizzie. And as far as knowing how to talk to boys, the best way to do that is to practice."

"Really?"

"I'm sure of it," she said. "And you're not the only one who's nervous, you know. Just think of how tough it is for the boys. I bet Billy Watts wishes he could think of something interesting to say to *you*."

"I never thought of it that way."

Ralph came in with an armload of groceries then, and kept us laughing while we finished making the cookies. Ralph is a really sweet man with warm blue eyes and kind of a crinkly smile that lights up his whole face. Some people would say he's a little pudgy, but I like to think that he's shaped like a cookie jar. Gram is very happy with him, and even though I wasn't thrilled when she decided to marry him, I know that she made the right decision.

I didn't hear from Nancy until Sunday night, but I didn't expect to, because she was staying with her father in Detroit. I had just curled up in bed when the phone rang.

"You wouldn't believe what a weekend I just had!"

I scrunched the pillows behind my head. "What happened?"

"Well, first of all, my father dropped a bombshell on me."

I sat up. This sounded serious. "What kind of bombshell?" My mind was racing. Was her father getting remarried? That was always a possibility, but I knew it would upset Nancy. She always hopes, deep down, that somehow her parents will get back together.

"Get ready for this," she warned.

"I'm ready."

"My parents want me to take piano lessons."

"What?"

"You heard me," she said patiently.

"But why?" And you, of all people, I nearly added. Nancy is probably the most unmusical person I know. I sit next to her in chorus, and believe me, she doesn't know a sharp from a flat.

"They want to do something special for me."

"Special?" I hugged the pillow to my chest. "Special isn't piano lessons. Special is a trip to Disneyland or a puppy."

"That's exactly the way I feel," Nancy said unhappily. "But what can I do? They think that they're doing me a big favor. Neither one of them had the chance to take piano lessons when they were growing up, and I guess they've always regretted it."

I didn't know what to say. It was nice that Nancy's parents wanted to do something nice for her, but they were way off track. "Maybe it won't be so bad," I said, trying to cheer her up.

"I'll find out on Monday," she said, sounding more down in the dumps than ever. "I start taking from Mrs. Stoker."

"Mrs. Stoker!" The words were out before I knew it. Adam took lessons from her last summer, and only lasted three weeks.

"Do you know her?"

"Not exactly," I hedged. "I've heard about her, though."

"Is she nice?"

The moment of truth. "She's supposed to be an excellent teacher," I said, choosing my words very carefully. I was glad we were talking on the phone instead of in person, or Nancy would have caught on to me in a minute.

"I hope she starts out slow," Nancy said. "You know, music isn't my strong point."

Did I ever! But this wasn't any time for complete honesty. "I think she'll start you with really basic stuff," I said, trying to be encouraging. "You'll probably just have to do scales, or something like that. It will be easy, you'll see."

"I hope you're right. How'd you like to come with me? Monday after school, at three-thirty."

"Sure." The last thing I wanted to do was see Mrs. Stoker (after everything Adam had said), but I couldn't let Nancy face her alone.

"Great!" I forced myself to smile. That was another one of Tina's tips. She said if you smile on the phone, your voice will sound warm. I hoped I was doing it right.

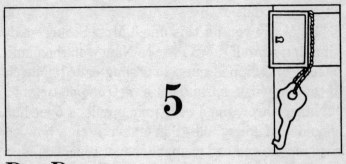

5

Dear Diary:

It's a good thing I went along with Nancy to her piano lesson today, or she would have backed out on the spot! Mrs. Stoker was just like Adam described her. A very large woman with bright pink hair the color of cotton candy. Nancy hung back when she ushered us into her living room and it was just as well. Mrs. Stoker's toy poodle went crazy the moment she saw us.

"Now, Fluffy," Mrs. Stoker said, scooping the poodle into her arms, "stop barking and say hello nicely to the girls."

"Hi there," Nancy said nervously. She hates small yappy dogs, and Fluffy must have caught on, because she suddenly bared her teeth and growled like a Doberman.

Everything went downhill from there. I sat stiffly on the edge of the sofa (with Fluffy eyeballing my every move) while Nancy perched on the piano bench. We exchanged a look while Mrs.

Stoker pawed through a big cardboard box filled with sheet music.

"Let's try you on this one," Mrs. Stoker said, plunking herself down next to Nancy on the piano bench. She flipped open to a song called "March of the Snowflakes," and set a metronome ticking.

Nancy threw me a *very* unhappy look over her shoulder. I knew she didn't have a clue how to read music, and had probably never touched piano keys in her life.

"I, uh, don't know much about the piano," she confessed.

Mrs. Stoker peered at her through lavender-tinted glasses. "You read music, don't you?"

Read music! I wanted to laugh. Nancy couldn't find middle C at gunpoint.

"Not really," Nancy said sheepishly.

"Oh dear, oh dear," Mrs. Stoker said. "I must have misunderstood what your mother said."

"Well, thanks anyway," Nancy said, all set to make her escape. She half stood up, only to find that Mrs. Stoker was in the way.

"Sit down," Mrs. Stoker said smilingly. "There's nothing to worry about. We'll just have to start from the very beginning, that's all. Sometimes it's better to have a student who doesn't know anything about the piano."

"It is?" Even Nancy had trouble believing that.

Mrs. Stoker bobbed her head enthusiastically.

"Oh yes, my dear. That way you don't have to unlearn any bad habits."

"Wonderful," Nancy said. She tried to smile, but she was gritting her teeth so hard, she didn't make it.

It was a little drizzly when Nancy and I finally walked home together.

"That was the longest hour of my life," she said feelingly.

"An hour and fifteen minutes," I pointed out. "Mrs. Stoker gave you an extra fifteen minutes because you're a new student."

Nancy flexed her fingers like she was trying on a pair of new gloves. "I'm absolutely sure I'm not cut out to play the piano. I hated every minute of that stupid lesson."

"It's too early to tell," I said, trying to think of something positive to say. Secretly, I had to agree with Nancy.

"I think Mrs. Stoker teaches mostly little kids."

I nodded. "I think so too. There was nothing to read in the whole place but *Humpty Dumpty* magazines."

Nancy giggled. "I meant the bit about 'thumbkin' and 'pinky.'"

"Oh that." I laughed, too. "Yeah, I thought I'd crack up when she named each one of your fingers."

"Are you *sure* Adam didn't say anything about her?"

"Well, he never stuck around long enough to get to know her. He only took lessons for three weeks."

"Three weeks!" We stopped for a red light, and Nancy thumped me hard in the ribs. "Why didn't you tell me?"

"Because I didn't want you to get off on the wrong foot with her. I wanted you to make up your own mind."

"Thanks a lot," Nancy muttered. We huddled together under a beat-up red umbrella until we reached my door.

"Want to come in? You can stay for dinner if you don't mind tofu burgers."

"Tofu burgers?"

"Dad's company is going into health foods. Especially vegetarian stuff." I paused, shifting from one food to the other. "The tofu burgers aren't too bad if you put a ton of ketchup on them. And if you don't look at what you're eating."

"Thanks, but I think I'll pass."

"Are you sure?"

"I'm sure. We're just having soup and sandwiches tonight because I need to get my notes in order."

"What notes?"

Nancy stared at me as if I had lost my mind.

"For Mr. Burrows's class! Don't you remember? He said we should bring in our note cards tomorrow so he can see how much progress we've made." She looked at me very hard. "You *have* made some progress, haven't you?"

"Of course," I said quickly. The rain was dripping off the edge of the umbrella and running down my nose. "A lot of progress."

"I'm glad," Nancy said, relaxing a little. "What's your topic?"

My brain stalled. "Um, it's on . . . on . . ."

"On . . . what?" Nancy prompted me.

Suddenly a page from my history book sprang to life. "On the Civil War." I said it so confidently, I almost convinced myself.

"That's good," she said approvingly. "You know, you really had me worried for a while. You took so long in getting started, I was afraid you wouldn't be able to come up with something."

"You worry too much," I told her. If she only knew!

Josh and Adam came barreling up the front steps then, and Nancy and I said good-bye. "Talk to you tonight," she said, dashing back into the rain.

"If I'm still alive after the tofu burger," I shouted after her.

Dinner went very quickly (mostly because no one felt like lingering over the Tofu Delights) and before I knew it, I was doing my homework.

I thought about the note cards that were due the next day, and wondered what to do. I'd either have to come up with something — fast — or make up an excuse to tell Mr. Burrows. Which would it be? I stood up and stretched and wandered over to the window. A light rain was falling against the roof, and I curled up on the window seat, staring out into the darkness. I love rainy nights, and sometimes I sit for hours, just listening to the sound, and smelling the sweet night air.

I started thinking about Billy Watts, and Tina's "tips" for talking to boys, and how Gram had said that I was a really interesting person. Of course, I could probably make myself even *more* interesting if I just practiced a little. Tina said that you should always have at least three funny stories in the back of your mind, so you can pull them out if there's a lull in the conversation. I cupped my chin in my hand and tried to think of even *one* funny story! Funny things happen to me, but usually they involve Nancy, and nobody else would even get them. Especially a boy . . .

The phone jangled and Nancy's voice jolted me back to reality. "I just wanted to talk for a second before I turn in," she said.

Turn in? I stared at the clock in surprise. It was nearly ten. I had been sitting at the window for ages, and now it was too late to get started on the note cards.

"I'm glad you called. What are you doing?" I said, settling back on the bed.

"Well, I finished my note cards," she said brightly. "Of course, everything is really rough and sketchy, but that's okay. Just so it gives Mr. Burrows some idea of what I'm doing." She paused, waiting for me to say something. "How are you doing?" she said finally. "Have you got your Civil War notes ready to go?"

"Pretty much." A huge lie if ever I heard one. I don't like fibbing to Nancy, but what else could I do? If I told her the truth, I'd get a lecture! Nancy can be pretty bossy when she wants to be, and she doesn't hesitate to tell me things "for my own good."

Nancy yawned just then. "How about if we finish this conversation tomorrow?" she said with a laugh. "I'm asleep standing up."

"Me too. Except I'm already lying down," I joked. "See you in the morning."

After I hung up, I tiptoed downstairs. The house was very quiet because everyone had turned in early, but I saw a light under Josh's door, and I knew he was watching TV. I made my way carefully to the den and took down a volume of the encyclopedia set Dad bought for Christmas a few years ago. Maybe I could find something to say about the Civil War, just enough to satisfy Mr. Burrows. Of course it would be better if I had done my "research" in the library,

35

but this would do in a pinch. I flipped through the pages and got more than I bargained for. There was tons of material on the Civil War! There were pages full of famous battles and a big discussion on the causes and effects. There was a whole section on slavery and the southern agricultural economy. I felt tired just looking at it. How could I pick a topic out of all this?

I curled up in the big wing chair in front of the TV, and very quietly grabbed the remote. It wouldn't hurt to take a quick peek at the TV. I changed channels until I found a horror movie and watched for a few minutes. It was a really old one, and the monster looked like he was wrapped in bedsheets. Then I switched to the home shopping channel, and finally found a late night cartoon. By this time, it was ten-thirty, and I knew I had to get to bed. I looked at the thick leather volume in my lap. Should I make a stab at doing the note cards? But it was already so late! Much too late to start such a big project. I decided I'd have to think of an excuse to tell Mr. Burrows in the morning.

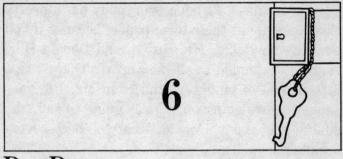

6

Dear **D**iary:

I was a nervous wreck today, and Tina's "tips" didn't help one little bit! (Tina said that if you act confident, you will actually start to feel confident. Hah! Fat chance.)

The day started out as a total disaster and ended up that way, too. I forgot to set my alarm, overslept, and had to scramble to get ready for school. I barely had time to pull on my oldest pair of jeans and a wrinkled T-shirt, when my shoelace snapped in half. What else could go wrong? Plenty! Darcy grabbed my umbrella before I could stop her, and I had to run five blocks in the pouring rain. Do you know what happens to naturally frizzy hair when water hits it? It's not a pretty sight. I looked like I was wearing a brillo pad with a permanent! And that was just the beginning. I never had a chance to think of a good excuse for Mr. Burrows, and before I knew it, nine o'clock history class had rolled around. As soon as the bell rang, Mr. Burrows said the words I had been dreading.

"Okay, boys and girls," he began, sitting on the edge of his desk. "I hope everybody has a pretty clear idea about their term paper, because if you don't by now . . ." He paused, and Donald Harrington pretended to slit his throat. There was a little ripple of laughter, and even Mr. Burrows smiled before going on. "I was going to say," he added, glancing at Donald, "that you better have a fantastic excuse."

A fantastic excuse. Just what I needed, I thought unhappily. But what could it be?

I watched Nancy arrange her note cards and rough draft pages into a neat pile on her desk. Everybody seemed to have *something* to show Mr. Burrows. Everybody except me.

"I'm going to stroll around the room," he said, starting down an aisle. "I'll talk to each of you individually, and in the meantime, I want everybody to read chapter fifteen." He paused and added in a deadpan voice, "It's a real winner. It's all about Grover Cleveland." This got the laugh he expected. I think sometimes Mr. Burrows likes to think he's a comedian.

I was glad to see that he was starting with Samantha Howard. As far as I could tell, her notes were a mess. She grabbed a handful of crumpled papers out of her purse and started frantically smoothing them out. Mr. Burrows took one look, and then folded his arms. "Maybe you'd better decipher these for me."

"Decipher?" Samantha had a way of tossing her head so her long blonde hair fell perfectly into place.

"Translate them." He held a piece of paper up to the light and squinted at it. "There's no way I can read this. It looks like a chicken scrawl."

A few kids giggled and Samantha reddened. "My pen ran out of ink. Anyway you said our papers didn't have to be in perfect shape for today. You just wanted to see what we were doing."

"So I did, Samantha," he said lightly. "And what exactly are you doing?"

"Well, I'm doing a paper on the Confederacy," she said smugly. "I've got an outline, sort of . . ." she added. She dug into her oversize purse again. "Here it is," she said triumphantly. "It doesn't have all those Roman numerals you told us about, but it's an outline." She paused and inspected her long fingernails. Mr. Burrows studied the paper for a minute or two. "Okay," he said finally, "it's a start. I see where you're heading, and it's not bad at all." Samantha looked very pleased with herself. "But I have a few suggestions . . ."

I flipped open my history book and pretended to be fascinated by the life and times of Grover Cleveland. I saw Nancy staring at me, and knew exactly what she was thinking. Where were my notes? My heart was thudding in my chest, as my brain scrambled for an excuse. The only one that came to mind was the old "I-left-my-notes-at-home." I thought it over for a minute, decided to give it a try, and then a strange thing happened. Donald Harrington and Alan Maggio said that they left *their* notes at home! Would Mr. Burrows believe it a third time? I held my breath as he moved down the aisle. The moment he reached Tanya Malone's desk, she said exactly the same thing! Now what could I do? He'd *never* believe it a fourth time.

My mind was an absolute blank when Mr. Burrows stood over me. I glanced at Nancy for help, but she shook her head and gave a helpless shrug.

"Well, Miss Miletti?" Mr. Burrows said. "Let's have a look at your notes." There was a definite edge to his voice. No doubt about it, he was annoyed. I simply *had* to think of something, and fast!

"They're . . . they're . . ." I studied the floor for a clue and then it came to me. "On computer," I finished brightly.

"On computer?" Mr. Burrows raised his eyebrows and Nancy's jaw dropped open. She knows that I feel the same way about computers that I do about brussels sprouts.

"Yes, and I'm afraid I didn't get a chance to print them out." I tried a little apologetic smile. "I ran out of computer paper late last night. I've got everything saved on the disk, though."

Mr. Burrows nodded sympathetically. Part of

40

me felt relieved, and part of me felt guilty at having tricked him. "I know what you mean, Lizzie. I've done the same thing myself." He started to move down the aisle, and then stopped and chuckled. "Just don't make a mistake and erase the disk. I've done *that* myself, too."

"Don't worry," I said merrily. "I'll be extra careful." The moment his back was turned, I looked at Nancy. She mouthed "What?" but I shook my head and buried my head in my history book. There would be time after class to make up a story for her.

When the bell rang half an hour later, I had a little surprise. Nancy was a lot harder to convince than Mr. Burrows! "Since when do you know how to use a computer?" she demanded as we headed toward English lit.

I put on my best "innocent" look. "Adam and Josh fool around with the computer every night after dinner. You know that. I was bound to pick up *something* just hanging around watching them."

"That's a little hard to believe," she said, wincing as Donald Harrington popped his bubble gum in her ear. "Especially since they play Nintendo."

Good point. "You'd be surprised at how much you can learn from playing computer games," I said seriously. "Skill, coordination . . ."

"Even word processing?" Darn. It was much

harder to fool Nancy than I thought.

"Um . . . well, I didn't say my notes were perfect. I just said they were on computer."

"So you did," she said. We whizzed into class just before the bell rang and luckily I didn't have to think up a reply.

I was glad that I had a chance to zip through dinner early that night. For once I had the perfect excuse — I had to meet Nancy at the library.

"I really hate to miss dessert," I said, glancing at a strange yellow blob that Mom put in the center of the table. It looked like a giant egg yolk and I watched as she spooned out portions for everybody. "Um, by the way, what is that?"

"Lemon Confetti Surprise," Dad said proudly. "It's new from our test kitchen at Roth. It's low-calorie, nearly fat-free, and completely microwavable in its own oven-to-table serving container. And it's recyclable."

"Oh, that's good." Dad always tells you more than you want to know.

"But what *is* it?" Adam asked in a whiney voice.

"It's a delicacy." Dad winked at me. "And just think, the Miletti family is one of the very first families in the country to try it."

"Maybe we'll be the last," Josh whispered to me. He waited until Dad wasn't looking, and then clutched his throat in a stranglehold and crossed his eyes.

Mom nudged him sharply in his side and shook her head. Even though she gets sick of serving weird frozen foods, she knows that Dad takes his business very seriously, and she doesn't want to hurt his feelings.

Dad seemed to be waiting for me to say something, so I took a quick bite before pushing back my chair.

"It's very . . . interesting, Dad. Really." It even *tasted* like a giant egg yolk. Disgusting! "And I like that part about the container being recyclable." I was already reaching for my jacket, all set to escape.

"Yeah, at least no trees had to give their lives," Adam hooted.

"Just a few humans," Josh said under his breath.

It was chilly when I crossed Front Street and headed up the library steps. Going to the library at night can either be extremely cool or extremely uncool, depending on a number of things. (Like who you are with, what you are wearing, what they are wearing, and whether or not you are going there to study.) Coolest of *all* is going to the library with a boy, and then going out for something to eat afterwards. I have no idea why this is so, but it just is.

This was obviously not going to happen to me tonight, because Nancy was already waiting for me at our favorite table by the window. She had on her "study" clothes (a navy blue sweatshirt with strange white bleach stains, and a pair of torn jeans) and had a pencil tucked behind her ear. She broke into a big grin when she saw me.

"Boy, have we got work to do!" she whispered loudly when I was a few feet away. I saw with a sinking feeling that she was buried under a pile of books and note cards. And she looked disgustingly happy. How did I ever get hooked up with a best friend who *loves* research!

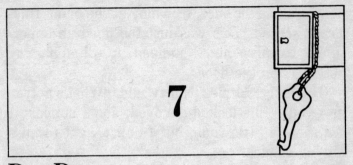

7

Dear **D**iary:

I faked my way through another long evening
at the library last night. I didn't plan it that way,
really. I had every intention of 1) telling Nancy
the truth about my nonexistent notes and 2) getting started on my term paper. But things got
way out of hand, and I ended up getting nothing
done. (You're probably thinking that it was all my
own fault, but you're only partly right.)

I would have been fine if Billy Watts hadn't
shown up. Really! I had just sat down with Nancy,
and was pretending to be interested in *her* term
paper, when I spotted Billy at the Info-Track machine. (The Info-Track is this amazingly cool computer that lets you find any book you want if you
punch in the right information.)

Nancy was right in the middle of telling me
more than I wanted to know about the Declaration
of Independence when Billy popped into view. He
looked great, as always, and was wearing a light
blue denim shirt and a pair of faded jeans. And

he was alone for once, frowning at the blank Info-Track screen. This was just too good an opportunity to miss, and I jumped up, dumping my notebook on the floor.

"Honestly, Lizzie," Nancy said. "What's gotten into you?" She looked annoyed, and I suppose I *did* seem a little rude, but I didn't want to miss my big chance!

"I'm sorry," I muttered, banging my shin sharply on the edge of my chair. "But I just had this super idea to add to my term paper, and I want to track it down before it gets away. You don't mind, do you?"

"Oh well, in that case . . ." She smiled and waved me on. "Go ahead, I can tell you the rest of the story later."

"Thanks," I said, my mind already on Billy. "I'll be back in a flash." I gave her my best "sincere" look before dashing down the aisle. Did I feel a little guilty about conning my best friend? You bet! But what else could I do? Nancy would *never* approve of talking to Billy Watts rather than working on a term paper.

Billy didn't hear me come up behind him, and he was busily tapping on the Info-Track. "I don't believe this," I heard him say. "I just don't believe it!"

"What's wrong?" I had hoped to sound really cool like Samantha Howard, but naturally my voice came out in a stupid squeak like Minnie Mouse.

"Oh, hi Lizzie." He looked up briefly, and then immediately ducked his head back to the machine. For some reason, he seemed totally at ease and not the least bit nervous.

I was definitely nervous. My knees felt wobbly and I grabbed the back of his chair. Was I doomed to act like an idiot every time I was around a cute boy?

"Well, I'm trying to find some reference books on Ben Franklin. I'm doing my term paper on his inventions," he went on to explain. "But would you believe there is *nothing* in the whole library about him? I typed in his name and got zilch!"

I shook my head in surprise and sat down next to him. "That's impossible," I said slowly. And then I figured it out. "Look, Billy, this is where you went wrong. You typed in 'Franklin, Benjamin,' but the machine wants you to say 'Benjamin Franklin.' "

"Are you sure?" He looked skeptical.

"Yeah, because I made the same mistake myself once. I don't know why it's set up that way, but it is." I pointed to the keyboard. "Try it out."

"Okay, here goes. I'm not a great typist," he said, after he messed up a few times.

"That's okay," I said sympathetically. "I've got plenty of time." If Nancy could only hear me! He

47

was successful after the fifth attempt and about a million references to Ben Franklin flashed on the screen.

"Wow, there's some dynamite stuff here. His inventions alone would fill a notebook."

"You'll have to narrow it down," I said, sounding just like Nancy. I read somewhere that best friends start to look alike and talk alike, but I never believed it until now. "Maybe just concentrate on a few of his inventions, and discuss them in detail."

"That's a good idea." He nodded very seriously.

I shrugged. "Well, I know that's what Mr. Burrows wants."

Billy started writing down book titles and then looked up, laughing. "Hey, what did you think of those clowns pretending to forget their notes the other day? Do you think Mr. Burrows fell for it?"

"I . . . uh, I'm not sure," I said.

"What a dumb excuse!" he howled. "How could anyone seriously try to get away with that?"

I smiled, trying to look very assured, the way Tina had suggested. "It beats me." I decided it was time to change the subject. Definitely. "I've got a great idea, Billy. Why don't you let me help you with this? I'll start looking for the books in the stacks while you get the authors and titles. That way you'll finish in half the time."

"Gosh, that's really nice of you." He hesitated.

"But aren't you pretty busy with your own paper?"

"Not really. I've got everything under control."

"It must be nice," he said enviously. "My notes were such a mess, I was really afraid to show them to Mr. Burrows. I guess you're a lot more organized than I am."

I tried to look humble. "Not really." And then I added in a burst of fantasy, "Having a computer really helps."

"Oh yeah, I forgot about that." He paused, his blue eyes serious. "I really appreciate your helping me like this."

I grinned. "No problem at all."

"I don't understand this one little bit," Nancy said flatly. It was two hours later, and they were announcing last call at the checkout desk. "You spent the whole time helping Billy Watts with his research?"

"Well, he was sort of in a bind," I said sheepishly. Nancy had caught me red-handed at the Info-Track with Billy half an hour earlier. "You see, he was having a lot of trouble using the Info-Track — "

"Of course, with your knowledge of computers, you could certainly fix that." At times, Nancy has a surprising talent for sarcasm.

"I don't claim to be an expert," I said modestly, "but I knew what he was doing wrong." I paused, wondering how much to tell her. "I just set him on the right track, that's all. He was very grateful."

"I bet." She didn't look taken in at all, and I realized I'd have to switch tactics fast.

"How did you do with George Washington? Don't forget I want to hear the rest of that story."

"It's a little late." She glanced at her watch. "Do you want to stop and get a soda, or do you need to get home to type up your notes?"

Type up my notes? "I'd love to get a soda," I told her.

"And you're sure you've got the time?" She was already heading to the checkout desk, loaded down with books and magazines.

I nodded. "All the time in the world."

It was very late when I got home. The house was quiet, and Mom was waiting up in the kitchen. She was wearing her favorite flannel bathrobe and was reading the paper.

"Do you believe it?" she said, sipping a cup of tea. "This is the first chance I've had to sit down all day." She paused and looked at me. "Do you ever have one of those days, when you can't seem to accomplish anything?"

Do I ever! I longed to say. "I guess so," I said mildly. I stifled a yawn. It was very late to start working on my term paper, but what could I do? Mr. Burrows was expecting *something* tomorrow.

I couldn't use the old computer-paper routine twice. And my brain refused to come up with something new.

"Oh, that reminds me. Nancy called a couple of minutes ago. You don't have to call her back, but she wants you to go to her piano lessons tomorrow."

"It's tomorrow?" I groaned. I didn't think I could take "March of the Snowflakes" the following day.

Mom looked surprised. "Is that a problem?"

"No," I said hastily. "No problem." I poured a glass of milk and headed up the stairs. "I better turn in. I've got a big day tomorrow."

"Night, sweetie," she called after me.

8

Dear **D**iary:

At three o'clock Mr. Burrows was frowning at me across the desk. "Still no computer paper, Lizzie?" he asked. He had told four of us to "see him after school," which is never good news from a teacher. Of course I knew exactly what he wanted. Our term paper notes! Both Donald Harrington and Alan Maggio handed him a few scribbled pages, and Tanya came up with a dozen or so index cards. Everybody was off the hook. Everybody but me!

"I . . . just didn't get to the store," I said. "But tomorrow, for sure." I jokingly held up my fingers in the boy scout pledge. "Scout's honor."

"Mmm." Mr. Burrows gave me a skeptical look. "I hope so, young lady." He checked his watch. "Why don't you go buy some paper right now. You could try Harrison's down on Main Street."

"Good idea," I said, scooping up my books. Nancy was waiting for me in the hall, and I could see her shifting from one foot to the other. "See you tomorrow."

"With the notes," he said pointedly.

I tried to look a little wounded. "Of course, Mr. Burrows."

"What did he say?" Nancy looked worried as we skipped down the steps. I wondered if she suspected what was going on.

"He just wanted to remind me to turn in my notes tomorrow. It's no big deal."

"But if he asked you to see him after class . . . Lizzie, you don't think this will affect your grade, do you?"

"Of course not." I punched her lightly in the arm. "Talk about worrying too much! Look, I'll get it done tonight. I'll go right home after your piano lesson and print them out. Okay?"

"Okay." She took a deep breath. "Do you think Mrs. Stoker will notice that I haven't practiced all week?"

I nodded very seriously. "She'll notice, that's for sure. And she might even hit thumbkin with that ruler she keeps next to her."

Nancy giggled. "Thanks a lot! I thought best friends were supposed to make each other feel better."

I shrugged. "Do you want the truth, or do you want to feel better?"

"Gee, when you put it that way, I'm not so sure."

It was just after three-thirty when we got to Mrs. Stoker's. Fluffy was lying in wait for us, pretending to be asleep under the piano.

"I expect great things of you today," Mrs. Stoker said to Nancy. Nancy managed to roll her eyes for my benefit, while Mrs. Stoker rummaged through her sheet music. "And once you get 'March of the Snowflakes' down pat, I've got a real treat in store for you. We're going to move right into 'Terry Tubas Triplets.' "

Nancy managed a weak smile. "That sounds great. But I had a little trouble with this 'Snowflake' piece . . ."

"You did?" Mrs. Stoker settled herself on the piano bench, and Nancy nearly toppled off the edge. "I'm surprised. Let's see what you've done with it."

I tuned out for the next hour, and watched Fluffy carefully gnaw her way through Nancy's shoelace.

The term paper notes were still nagging at me. What would I do for tomorrow? I couldn't stall forever.

Fluffy had come to life and was barking her head off as Nancy picked up her books from the sofa. "Let's get *out* of here," she said under her breath.

At the end of the hour, Mrs. Stoker said, "Remember dear, practice, practice, practice."

"Oh, I will," Nancy answered, practically pushing me through the door. "See you next week." The minute we were down the steps she took a deep breath. "I thought that would *never* end. These stupid piano lessons are going to kill me. And I'm not getting any better." She stopped and looked at me. "You know I'm not. Admit it."

"How do you expect to ever get any better if you don't practice?"

Nancy sighed. "You sound just like Mrs. Stoker." She checked her watch and grabbed my elbow. "It's still early," she said. "What do you say to an ice-cream float at the Zephyr? My treat."

I breathed a sigh of relief. She had completely forgotten that I was supposed to go buy computer paper. "I say you're on!"

"Look at my fingers," she said half an hour later. We were settled in a back booth at the Zephyr, which is our favorite ice-cream hangout.

"What's wrong with them?"

"They look like claws. I don't think I can unbend them." She carefully stretched her fingers one by one. "Mrs. Stoker made me keep them clenched for so long, I think they're locked this way forever."

"Of course they're not," I giggled. "I noticed she jabbed thumbkin with the ruler every time he got out of position, though."

"You know, I've come to a decision," Nancy said thoughtfully. She was playing with the straw in her ice-cream float, and her expression was serious. "I think I'm going to have to take this piano thing seriously, and really start practicing. Otherwise, I'm just wasting my parents' money for lessons. And it's not fair."

I nodded. "It's too bad you don't even *like* taking lessons."

"I know, but my parents think it's the right thing for me to do. So the least I can do is put some effort into it."

Nancy tends to take things very seriously, and I knew she would do exactly what she said. She was about to say more, but Ericka Powell came in just then and plopped down next to us. Ericka is a really nice girl from Alaska, and I guess the best way to describe her is to say she's very calm and sane. If there was ever an emergency, you'd probably want to have someone like Ericka around. She ordered a black cow and ate it so fast she practically inhaled it.

It was late when we left the Zephyr, but we stopped for a quick hamburger in the mall anyway. I called Mom for permission first, and she said it was okay if I got home by seven-thirty. Usually Mom and Dad like all of us to eat dinner together, but lately everybody tends to scatter in different directions. Adam and Josh are involved in a lot of sports, Darcy belongs to a scout troop, and even Rose belongs to a play group. So sometimes Mom has dinner with Dad alone, and keeps everything hot for us.

Tonight Mom was sitting at the kitchen table with Gram, and I hugged both of them. Usually Gram doesn't come over on weeknights, and I was glad to see her.

"Have some dessert with us," Mom said. "Apple crisp with whipped cream." She lowered her voice. "And it's *not* from Roth's Frozen Foods. Gram made it."

"Wow, then I know it's good."

Mom made a pot of tea and the three of us talked for over an hour. Gram told us lots of funny stories about her real estate job, and I could have sat there forever, except Mom suddenly asked me if I had any homework. Homework! Why is that always the last thing on my mind? I needed to get started on my term paper. This time for real!

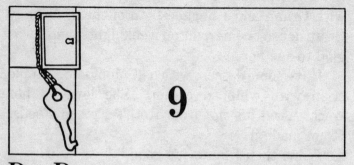

9

Dear **D**iary:

I can't believe it! I'm off the hook with Mr. Burrows! (At least for the moment.) I caught him in the hall right before class today and began a bumbling apology.

"Mr. Burrows, about those notes . . ." I had barely gotten the words out when he said that the rough draft was due in a few weeks, and I could hold off until then. Talk about luck! I'm beginning to think that timing is everything in life. I managed to catch him just as he was talking to Ms. Basley, my homeroom teacher, and I guess he didn't want to be interrupted. Anyway, I feel about ten pounds lighter!

Luckily, Nancy missed the whole thing because she was in gym class. I decided that it's easier to let her *think* that I turned in my notes (and that I'm plugging away on the term paper). After all, I have *ages* to get it done and there's no reason to have her nag at me. . . .

Nancy is having her own problems, because Mrs. Stoker just told her that she expects her to play in a piano recital with a bunch of little kids! How embarrassing. I would die if that happened to me, but naturally I had to act like it wasn't such a bad idea.

"It's not the end of the world, you know."

"Get serious. I'll look like an idiot," she wailed. It was three-thirty, and we were sitting in my kitchen. "How would you like to play 'March of the Snowflakes' for a whole room full of people? And as a duet!"

"I don't know. It might be good experience," I said slowly.

"Good experience?" Nancy looked at me as if I had lost my mind. "For what — playing in Carnegie Hall?"

I felt like giggling, but I managed to keep a straight face. "No, I just meant that it's a good idea to have to play for other people. That way you have a goal to work toward."

The phone rang, and I was amazed to hear a little kid on the other end ask for Nancy.

"It's for you," I said.

"Very funny."

"No, it really is." I lowered my voice. "A girl with a squeaky little voice like a talking Barbie doll."

Nancy frowned and took the receiver. She lis-

59

tened for a minute, raised her eyebrows, nodded a lot, and finally mumbled something I couldn't understand. Then she hung up.

"Well?" I knew something important had happened because two little pinpoints of red suddenly jumped out on Nancy's cheeks.

"You're not going to believe this," she said slowly.

"Try me."

"I don't even believe it myself." She took a deep breath and faced me. "That was Cindy Howard."

A light bulb went on in my brain. "Cindy Howard. You mean — "

"Samantha Howard's little sister."

"You're kidding! Why was she calling you? And why here?"

"She's . . . she's . . . oh, I just can't face it!"

The suspense was driving me crazy, and I jumped to my feet. If I had to, I was going to *shake* the truth out of Nancy. "What is it?" I yelled.

"She's my partner for the piano recital at Mrs. Stoker's." The words came out in a rush.

"Cindy Howard?"

"I know it makes no sense, but it's true," Nancy said miserably. She sunk into the kitchen chair. "Mrs. Stoker gave her my name, and Samantha said she'd probably find me over here."

"Wow, I can't believe it." It wasn't the brightest

thing in the world to say, but I was in shock. It was bad enough to have to play a duet with a little kid, but Cindy Howard! If she was anything like her sister, it would be a disaster.

"She wants me to come to her house after dinner tonight. So we can start rehearsing."

"Oh no." I stared at Nancy. There was no need for words. Both of us knew exactly what the other was thinking.

"Come with me," she said softly. "Please."

I nodded. "Of course." I thought briefly of my term paper, and pushed the thought aside. This was no time to think about history. This was an emergency!

The evening went just as badly as I had expected.

"C'mon in. You're right on time." Samantha looked terrific as usual in pink-and-black spandex biking gear. She gave us the once-over, and gestured toward the living room. There was an enormous grand piano in the corner, and a little kid dressed in designer jeans was playing scales.

"Cindy," Samantha yelled, "quit playing for a minute. Your . . . um . . . partner's here." She snickered a little during the last sentence, and I wondered if Nancy noticed.

"Oh, finally," Cindy answered. She gave a very dramatic sigh and walked across the room to greet us. "I've been practicing *forever*, and my fingers are absolutely *numb!*" Nancy and I exchanged a look. It was amazing how much Cindy resembled her sister. She had everything down pat, from the whiney voice to the blonde-on-blonde streaked hair. She dressed just like her, too, and I noticed that her knit top was right out of the pages of *Seventeen.*

"Well, shall we get started?" she asked, taking control of the situation right away. "Which one of you is Nancy?"

"Not me," I said gratefully, sinking into an easy chair. I didn't envy Nancy one little bit. A rehearsal with Cindy was going to be worse than an hour with Mrs. Stoker!

"So what are you doing here?" Samantha asked me. "Just tagging along with Nancy? You must have a lot of free time on your hands."

"Not really," I said, feeling a little embarrassed. Samantha loves to make people feel totally uncool, and has a real knack for it. "Actually, I've got a lot to do tonight."

Samantha raised her eyebrows. "Really," she said, inspecting a frosted beige fingernail. "You must mean school stuff."

"Well, that, too," I answered. I stared at the TV screen, and pretended to be interested in the news. "Actually, I was thinking of going to the mall after we leave here. I'm dying to get some new jeans." I had no idea where that came from, but sometimes I babble when I'm nervous or embarrassed.

Samantha shrugged. "I'm going there right now with Candace and Jessica. I'd ask you to go with us, but you know how it is." She gave me a phoney smile, as if she was really sorry she couldn't invite me.

"That's okay," I said coolly. "I wouldn't want to go without Nancy."

"Oh yeah, I forgot. You two are like Siamese twins." She gave a nasty little laugh. She jumped up when a car horn tooted outside. "There's my ride," she said, dashing to the door. "Have fun," she tossed over her shoulder to Nancy and Cindy.

I settled down to watch the news, but I couldn't tune out the sounds of Cindy and Nancy rehearsing. The two of them didn't hit it off at all, and Cindy seemed to have Samantha's talent for put-downs.

"Honestly," she whined, "how do you expect me to play the melody part, if you keep messing up on the harmony?"

"The harmony?" It was obvious that Nancy had no idea what Cindy was talking about.

"The left hand part," Cindy said icily. "The chords. Or don't you play chords yet?"

"Um, chords, let me think." Nancy squinted and stared into space as if she was trying hard to remember something. "Oh, now I get it," she said brightly, "chords are when you play a lot of keys at once."

Cindy muttered something I couldn't catch, and shook her head. "How long have you been taking from Mrs. Stoker?"

"About three weeks."

"Oh wow, I *really* got stuck this time," Cindy said very seriously. "I thought last year was the worst, when Mrs. Stoker made me play with Dirk Owen."

"Who's Dirk Owen?"

"It doesn't matter. He's just some kid who is absolutely tone-deaf. We played a Mexican song together, and he never even noticed when I turned the page."

"You mean he played by ear?"

"Hah!" Cindy snorted. "He couldn't even read music. He played the same bass chord over and over. Like this." She pounded the piano keys with her fist and I winced. "It didn't even go with the song!"

"Yeah, I see what you mean." Nancy rubbed her ear. "So what do you think we should do?"

Cindy tapped her fingers against the piano keys. "Well, unless you want to make a complete idiot out of yourself, I guess you'll really have to practice."

"Maybe we could just tell Mrs. Stoker that the song's too hard for me?" Nancy looked hopeful.

"No way." Cindy shook her head. "She gets really mad when kids do that. She says she spends hours picking just the right song for each student, and that she knows what we can handle. What a laugh! She sure didn't know what Dirk Owen could handle."

Nancy stared at the music for a minute. "But you really think I'll be able to do it? If I practice, I mean."

"I think so," Cindy said slowly. "Don't take this the wrong way, but I don't think you're super-talented. You'll have to work harder than most of the kids just to get through it."

"Yeah, I think you're right."

"How come you're taking piano lessons anyway?"

Nancy made a face. "My parents think it's a great idea."

"Really? Mine too." She paused. "I wanted to take ballet lessons instead. I've always wanted to be a ballerina, haven't you?"

Nancy glanced over her shoulder when she heard me giggle. "Um, not exactly," she said. "I don't think dancing is one of my strong points, either."

"Yeah? Well, maybe not." Cindy gave a heavy sigh. "I guess we should get back to the piano.

Now about these chords . . . do the words *major*
and *minor* mean anything to you?"

Nancy looked apologetic. "Not a thing," she
admitted.

Cindy stared at the ceiling for a moment, and
shook her head wordlessly. "Another Dirk Owen,"
she said after a moment. "Boy, do we have work
to do!"

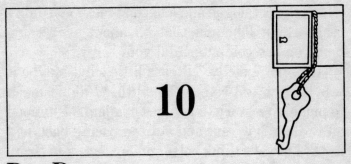

10

Dear **D**iary:

Have you ever noticed that the more you try to forget something, the more it stays on your mind? That's exactly what happened with my term paper. Even though I did my best to ignore it, it kept cropping up like a jack-in-the-box.

Of course, it didn't help that Nancy talked about *her* term paper all the time. (And would ask me little nagging questions about *mine* whenever she got the chance.) I knew she was suspicious, and last Saturday morning, we finally had it out.

"You haven't even started on your paper yet, have you?" Nancy was flopped on my bed thumbing through a Land's End catalogue, and she caught me off guard.

"What makes you say that?"

"Because you get very quiet whenever I mention it. It's a real giveaway, you know."

"Oh." It's very hard to lie to Nancy. "Maybe I'm just not interested in talking about it."

I saw from her face that she didn't buy it. She

closed the catalogue and looked at me. "You didn't really think I bought that bit about everything being on the computer, did you?"

"Um, not exactly." I felt a little silly. Maybe it was time to tell Nancy the truth. "I didn't mean to make up a story, but I was in a jam." I jumped off the window seat and started pacing back and forth. I always think better on my feet, and Gram says she's the same way, so maybe it runs in the family. "I had to come up with an excuse for Mr. Burrows, and that was the first thing I could think of."

"So you really haven't started on it — not at all?" Nancy looked worried, and that made me feel a little edgy.

"Well, hey, there's plenty of time, you know." I gave a little laugh that didn't quite come off. "You know me. I can always pull something out of the hat at the last minute."

"Not a term paper, you can't! It takes weeks to do it right." Before I even realized what was happening, Nancy shoved my jacket at me and was pushing me toward the door.

"What's going on?"

"We're going to the library," she said grimly. "And this time, there will be no excuses. I mean it, Lizzie Miletti, not one!"

What happened next is not to be believed! I know you'd like to think that I went to the library, and found a great topic for my term paper, and buried myself in a bunch of reference books. And I guess it *could* have happened that way, but it didn't.

This is the way it really happened. The library was jammed with kids, and it took us nearly five minutes to find two seats together at a table near the checkout desk. Nancy waited till I sat down and then glanced at her index cards.

"Don't move," she said sternly. "I'll only be gone a minute. I need to check a couple of references."

"Where would I go?" I said innocently.

"I don't know," she admitted. "Just don't get any ideas."

"Honestly, Nancy, you're so suspicious."

"Hah!" She tossed the last word over her shoulder before moving away.

I was sitting there for about ten seconds, tapping my pencil idly on the table, when someone grabbed me from behind.

"Lizzie Miletti! Ohmigosh, I can't believe it's really you!"

I struggled out of a kind of backwards bear hug to see Trina Edwards smiling at me. "Trina! I can't believe it's you either. What are you doing back in town?"

Trina and her twin sister, Terry, and I were bunkmates at the Lazy Corral summer camp three years ago. We haven't seen each other since then, although we exchange Christmas cards.

Trina slid into Nancy's seat and I closed my notebook. "We're just here for a couple of days because my mom is visiting her cousin. It's so neat to see you!"

"You, too!" I wasn't just being polite. It *was* great to see her. Trina has red hair, a million freckles, and can crack me up just by ordering a hamburger. She's one of those people who doesn't even have to try to be funny. She just is!

"So have you been horseback riding lately?" The moment I said this, Trina went into gales of laughter. I should explain that this was an "in" joke at the Lazy Corral. All of the new kids were so sore from horseback riding that they could hardly walk. So whenever anyone staggered into the dining room at night, we'd ask if they had "been horseback riding lately." (You'd probably have to be there to think it's really funny.)

"You remembered!" Trina squealed happily. "Say, do you remember the time Anthony Morris fell off his horse, and the counselor never even noticed? I mean, talk about funny!"

"Yeah, but don't forget when the tent collapsed on us in that thunderstorm and Terry slept right through it!"

"How could I?" Trina hooted. "Terry hasn't changed a bit. Hey, she's right outside in the car. Do you want to see her?"

"Well, I really shouldn't . . ."

"Oh, of course you can." Trina pleaded. "You're not doing anything important, are you?"

"Well, I . . ."

I'm not sure what would have happened next if Miss Simmons, the reference librarian, hadn't come over at that exact moment. (I'd like to say that I would have stayed and worked on my term paper, but I have to be completely honest. I just don't know.)

"Girls," she said, putting her hands firmly on Trina's shoulder, "you're making an awful lot of noise. Either keep it down, or please step outside to do your talking."

"Sorry," Trina and I muttered in unison. I glanced down the table. A couple of kids were giving us dirty looks.

"C'mon," Trina said, standing up. "She's right. We really can't talk here."

"No, I'm not sure . . ."

"Of course you are," Trina giggled and pulled me to my feet. "Terry will never forgive me if I don't bring you out to see her."

"Well, maybe just for a minute," I said, weakening. I knew Nancy would kill me, but what could I do? It might be another three years before I saw Trina and Terry again.

"Bring your books," Trina said. "My mom's taking us for a snack at that croissant place up the street."

"La Boulangerie? I've been dying to go there."

"Then come with us."

"Uh . . . I guess I could. Just for a little while. The trouble is, I'm with a friend. But I don't know where she is."

Trina shrugged. "So leave a note. We'll only be gone half an hour. I promise."

"You're sure?"

"I'm sure."

You can probably guess what happened next, Diary, because you know me so well. We were gone two-and-a-half hours! How is that possible? Well, we had a million things to say to each other, and Mrs. Edwards likes to talk as much as her daughters do. (And she's just as funny.) Between the three of them, I could hardly get a word in edgewise. Trina and Terry wanted to know if I had seen any of the kids from camp, and I wanted to hear all about what life was like in their new town. I can't really explain what happened to the time except to say that it just slipped away!

I was shocked to see that the sky had gotten dark by the time we left the mall, and Mrs. Edwards offered to drive me home.

"I was planning on going back to the library," I began, and then looked at my watch. What was I saying? The library was closed. Nancy would be furious. "But I'll go home instead," I said, already preparing for the worst.

I was right. Nancy was furious. When Nancy

gets really mad, she gets very quiet, which is what happened when I called her to apologize.

"Nancy," I said timidly, "are you still there?"

"I'm here," she said flatly.

"Good, I was afraid for a minute there you had hung up."

"Is there anything else you want to say?" Her voice was very cool.

"Not really. I just wanted to explain what happened. You see, I hadn't seen Trina and Terry in ages, and who knows when I'll see them again."

"Yes, you said that." Very cool. Very flat.

"So, uh, well, I just wanted to make sure you understood. . . ."

"I understand more than you think, Lizzie Miletti. And I just want you to know that from now on, you are on your own with your term paper. I give up!"

"Aw, c'mon, Nancy . . ."

"No, I mean it, Lizzie. I'm not going to remind you anymore, or try to talk you into working on it. From now on, it's sink or swim!"

And then she hung up. I sighed and got ready for bed. Nancy and I never stay mad at each other for long, and I knew that everything would be okay by the next day. Still, I couldn't forget her words ringing in my ear. Sink or swim? Surely the situation wasn't that desperate. I had *plenty* of time to get my term paper done. What was the big deal, anyway?

73

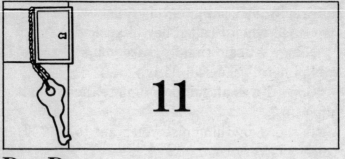

11

Dear **D**iary:

The past three weeks have been incredibly busy, and I've sort of let my work slide. But don't worry, Diary, because I know I can get caught up once Nancy's recital is over. She had another rehearsal with Cindy today and had a bad case of the jitters.

"I'm trembling like a leaf," Nancy whispered. "If Samantha snickers at me, I won't even be able to hit the keys."

"Don't be silly, just ignore her. Anyway, it's just a rehearsal, and you know what the drama teacher always says. If you have a bad rehearsal, it means you're going to give a great performance."

"Yeah?" Nancy looked skeptical.

"Absolutely." Actually, I wasn't at all sure the rule applied to piano recitals, but there was no sense in making Nancy feel worse than she already did.

"Did you bring a book to read?"

I held up a book on Civil War battles. "Of

course. Do you think I want to spend the whole time watching *Gilligan's Island* reruns?"

"*Please* try to get something done on your term paper."

"Of course I will." I did my best to look hurt. "Don't you think I know the rough draft is due on Monday?"

Nancy looked at me very seriously. "Knowing when it's due, and doing something about it are two different things."

"Did anyone ever tell you that you worry too much?"

Nancy never got a chance to reply, because Samantha opened the door just then. She was wearing a trendy new outfit I hadn't seen before, a clingy black top, with white jeans and black cowboy boots. She looked less than thrilled to see us.

"You're here again?" she said, raising her eyebrows.

"Practice makes perfect," I muttered as we swept past her into the living room.

Cindy barreled down the stairs at that moment, and she seemed genuinely glad to see Nancy.

"Hi, partner," she said with a big grin. "Do you think you have those major chords down pat?"

"I even did the minor ones," Nancy said proudly. "I practiced for hours last weekend."

Samantha snorted. "It must be nice to have so much time on your hands."

Cindy looked up from the piano. "Hey, I'm glad Nancy's working on her music," she said sharply. "She was so bad in the beginning, I thought I was going to have play both parts myself." She turned to Nancy apologetically. "I didn't mean that the way it sounded."

"That's okay. I know I was really awful the first day I came over here."

"Yeah, well, you're lots better now," Cindy said agreeably. "Let's get started, okay? Remember that it's four-four time, and don't rush the beginning. That always makes Mrs. Stoker crazy."

"Don't I know it!"

I tuned out the rest of the rehearsal and turned my attention to my big fat book on the Civil War. Why had I chosen such an enormous one? I wondered. I felt tired just thinking about all the dates and names inside it!

I tried to ignore Samantha who was sitting across from me, thumbing through a fashion magazine.

"What do you think of these leather chaps they're wearing in California?" she said out of the blue.

"Leather chaps?" I had no idea what she was talking about. I vaguely remembered hearing that chaps were something horses wore, like a bridle. "You mean for people?" I asked stupidly.

She rolled her eyes and held up the magazine.

"Of course I mean for people! They're the latest thing on the West Coast. Honestly, sometimes I think you and Nancy must live in a cave. You never have any idea what's going on."

I winced. I do try to keep up with the new styles. I don't dress like Samantha, but I don't look like a mess either.

"Take a look at this," Samantha urged, passing me a magazine. The girl on the cover was dressed like a rock star, in black leather and metal mesh. "What do you think of it?"

I took a deep breath. "Awful. The pits."

"Yeah?" Samantha said slowly. She looked at the magazine again. "You know something? You're absolutely right. But these French lace jeans are cool. Of course, they *should* be, for four hundred dollars."

"I can't understand it," Nancy said later, as we walked home together. "You and Samantha were chattering away like you were buddies or something."

"Not exactly," I said. "We just got talking about clothes, that's all."

"Oh, *clothes*," Nancy said, wrinkling her nose.

I decided to change the subject. I didn't want Nancy to start asking about my Civil War book, which I hadn't even looked at.

She was too quick for me. "Did you get a lot of research done tonight?"

I gave a very realistic groan. "Tons. Absolutely tons."

She beamed and squeezed my arm. "That's good. I'm proud of you. You'll see, Lizzie. This paper will turn out even better than you planned."

I certainly hope so, I thought.

I don't know how to tell you the next part of the story except Monday crept up on me! Really. It just rolled around without my noticing. Well, almost.

This is what happened. On Sunday night, I zipped upstairs right after dinner and took the phone off the hook. That way I wouldn't even be *tempted* to waste my time talking. Smart, right?

Have you ever noticed how much noise a phone makes when it's off the hook? It drove me crazy! I wrapped it in a towel and I still could hear it beeping in my room. Finally I slammed it back on the hook, and of course it immediately started ringing.

First Gram called. "Hello dear. Did you know your phone was off the hook? I reported it to the operator."

Then my father called from the airport. "I've been trying to get your mother for half an hour! Who's been on the phone?"

Next, Mary Lou Witty called for Josh. (Mary Lou is his girlfriend and she goes into a panic if they don't speak to each other at least five times a night.)

I took two calls for Adam, followed by a wrong number, and then Nancy called. "You've been on the phone all night! I hope you're working on your paper."

Wow. Talk about a wasted evening. I looked at the clock, and somehow it was nine-thirty. Nine-thirty! Mom stuck her head in the door just as I was going to make a stab at my rough draft.

"Don't stay up too late, honey. You looked a little tired at dinner."

"I'm fine," I said automatically, and then stopped myself. "Actually, I *do* feel a little sick. I think I'm getting a cold."

"Really?" Mom used to be a nurse, and she immediately felt my forehead. "I don't think you have a fever, but you do look a little pale." She turned out my desk light. "Just get a good night's sleep and you'll be fine in the morning."

And then the idea hit me. It was so simple I don't know why I hadn't thought of it earlier. If I was sick, I couldn't go to school. And if I couldn't go to school, well, you get the rest of the picture. Fine was the last thing I was going to be in the morning. With any luck I would be at death's door!

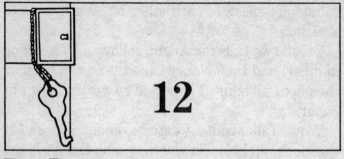

12

Dear **D**iary:

If they ever give out Academy Awards for playing sick, I should win one. The next morning, I ignored the alarm clock, burrowed under the covers, and waited for Mom to check on me.

"I don't think it's anything serious," she said, handing me a glass of orange juice. "Just a cold, or maybe a touch of that virus that's going around."

"I'll be fine, really." *In a day or two*, I added silently.

"You do look a little pale, but I think a day's rest will fix you right up."

"I think so, too." I smiled (weakly, of course) and settled back on the pillows. A day at home wouldn't be so bad, I decided. I knew Mom would make me stay in bed, but at least I could do a little reading, and maybe even think about my term paper. Nancy could get my homework for me, so I wouldn't miss any schoolwork. And best of all, I *would* miss seeing Mr. Burrows. I knew

I couldn't stall him off forever, but I was just going to take it one day at a time.

"What do you mean she's sick?" Adam said suspiciously. "She doesn't look sick to me." He poked his head in the door to give his diagnosis, and I made a face at him. For some reason, Adam can't stand it if anyone stays home sick. He always thinks they're faking it. (Okay, I know what you're thinking. I *was* faking it, but that's not the point.)

I dozed off for most of the morning, and by the time I got up and took a shower, it was late afternoon when Nancy stopped by with my homework.

"How *are* you?" she asked, sitting on the edge of my bed. Nancy is just the opposite of Adam, and always gives everyone the benefit of the doubt. Even if she was a tiny bit suspicious of me, she would never let on.

"Oh, I'm . . . doing much better," I said. I gave a little cough and reached for my assignments.

"Everyone said they hope you get well soon." She was staring hard at me, and I felt embarrassed. How had I ever gotten into this mess? I had lied to Mr. Burrows, my mother, and my best friend, all because of a term paper!

"I guess you need to do the math assignment because we're having a chapter quiz on Friday," she began. "And we're supposed to read the first thirty pages of *Silas Marner* . . . and oh yeah, guess what?"

81

"What?" I glanced at the math assignment. It had so many numbers and squiggles, it could have been the directions for a moon landing.

"Mr. Burrows is going to be gone all next week."

"What?" I was so shocked, I nearly tumbled out of bed.

"That's right. He's been invited to speak at some big teacher's conference in Ohio."

"Wow." Things were working out even better than I had hoped. "So I guess we can turn our term papers in late," I said slowly.

"Oh no, it doesn't change anything." Nancy looked disgustingly cheerful. "In fact, he reminded us that he wants them the day he gets back. The Monday after next."

The Monday after next! Somehow hearing the word brought it home to me. The term papers were due next week, and I was going to have to come up with something. But what? I needed time alone to think things over.

"You know, Nancy," I said leaning back on the pillow. "I've got this awful headache . . ."

"Oh, I'm sorry," she said, jumping up. "I probably shouldn't have stayed so long."

"No, that's okay. But I think I need to rest for a while."

"Sure, I understand. Just try and take it easy." She paused, and I knew she had something on her mind. "I need to get home and practice, anyway. I've got a big weekend coming up." she said a little shyly. "The piano recital, you know."

"Gosh, I completely forgot." I felt like a jerk. Nancy had told me the date a dozen times. "I'll go with you."

"Are you sure you'll be okay by then?" Just the way she said it made me realize how much she wanted me to be there.

"I'm positive." I sank back on the pillows. "Don't worry about a thing."

The moment she left, I jumped out of bed. I had a math assignment that would stump a rocket scientist, an entire term paper to write, and a splitting headache that was *real*. Things were totally out of control! I decided to tackle the math problems first. The term paper would just have to wait. . . .

Before I knew it, the weekend had rolled around. It was the day of Nancy's piano recital, and my stomach felt like someone's butterfly collection had just moved in. Why was *I* so nervous?

"You look great," I whispered to Nancy before the program started. She had gotten very dressed up (for Nancy) and was wearing a navy blue cotton skirt with a new white turtleneck, and dark blue flats. We were sitting side by side on metal folding chairs in Mrs. Stoker's living room. I noticed that practically all the kids there were under eight years old, but decided not to point this out. Nancy's parents were sitting in the row behind us.

"I just hope I can get through this," Nancy whispered. "Mrs. Stoker said that everybody gets stage fright, but that once you sit down at the piano, it goes away."

"Well, I'm sure she knows what she's talking about." I tried to look encouraging, but I had my doubts. The last time I had to read a book report in English class, my knees shook the entire time I was talking. "Anyway, you'll have so much to think about, you won't have time to get nervous."

That was the wrong thing to say. Nancy frowned and clutched my arm in sudden panic. "Ohmigosh, I just thought of something. What if I forget the whole piece? What if I can't remember my part? What if I go blank?"

"Nancy, please," I said, gently loosening her hand from my sleeve. "I didn't mean it that way. Of course you're not going to forget the piece. You've played it a dozen times. You could probably play it in your sleep."

"Yeah, I guess you're right." Nancy closed her eyes and leaned back for a moment. "In fact, I have played it in my sleep. I dreamt about this moment all last night."

Just then, Nancy's partner, Cindy Howard, looked our way and gave a little wave. She was sitting with her parents, and I was glad to see that Samantha wasn't with them.

"Look how calm she looks," Nancy said admiringly. "I wish I could be like that."

"What's the big deal?" A little girl in a white crinoline dress turned around to stare at us. She didn't look a day over six years old. "We go through this twice a year."

"You do?"

She nodded, her blonde curls bouncing. "I've been doing this since I was four." She glanced at Nancy. "You're kind of old to be here. What are you playing?"

" 'Mexican Hat Dance.' As a duet."

The little girl hooted. "That's baby stuff. I can't believe you got stuck with that."

Before Nancy could think of a reply, we heard a loud snicker behind us. I glanced over my shoulder and groaned.

"Oh no," I said softly. "They're here."

Samantha, Jessica, and Candace made a big entrance, happy that everyone noticed them.

"Excuse me," Samantha said more loudly than was necessary. She settled down right behind us, and tapped me on the shoulder. "Gee, I didn't expect to see you at a kiddie recital. You must — "

"I know, I know, I must have a lot of time on my hands," I said, cutting her off.

"Hi Nancy," Jessica and Candace said in unison. They exchanged a look and burst out laughing. "Maybe you'll get a lollipop if you don't mess up."

"Very funny," I muttered. I looked over at Nancy who was *looking* a little green. "Are you okay?" I asked her.

"I feel awful," she whispered. "I'm sick to my stomach and the room is sort of swimming. I think I'm going to — "

"Don't even say it," I said, surprising both Nancy and myself. "You are not going to be sick, Nancy Underpeace, so don't even think about it."

"I'm not?" She looked miserable.

"No, you are not." I sounded a lot more certain than I really felt. "You are going to take three deep breaths, and you are going to go up there and do a great job."

"I'll try," she said shakily.

A few moments later, Mrs. Stoker walked to the front of the room and the program started. Nancy gripped my hand so tightly my fingers were tingling, but I managed to give her a big smile.

"Remember, three deep breaths," I whispered.

She nodded, licking her lips over and over like a nervous cat on its way to the vet.

When her name was called, along with Cindy Howard's, there was a smattering of applause from the row behind us.

"Knock 'em dead, Nancy," Samantha said nastily, and her friends giggled.

"We should have brought a tape recorder," Jessica hooted.

Nancy made her way unsteadily toward the piano, where Cindy was already waiting, hands poised over the keys. She glanced my way as she sat down, and I gave her a thumbs-up sign. My heart was beating like a rabbit's, and I crossed my fingers.

There was a long silence while Nancy stared at the keys, and Cindy shifted on the piano bench. For one awful second I wondered if she was going to get through it. Then suddenly Nancy took a deep breath, nodded to Cindy, and hit the keys. The sounds of "Mexican Hat Dance" flooded the room and everybody stopped rustling their programs to listen.

I nearly giggled in relief. Nancy was great! She never missed a note, and even Cindy glanced at her once or twice in surprise. When it was over, she took a little bow and walked back to her seat.

"You did it!" I said, hugging her.

"I'm so glad it's over," she said, hugging me back. "But it wasn't as bad as I thought it would be. In fact, it was kind of fun."

"Really? Then how about an encore?" I teased her.

She punched me lightly in the arm. "An encore? You've got to be kidding!"

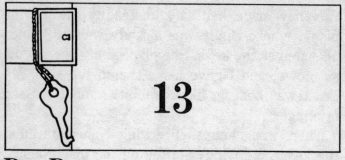

13

Dear **D**iary:

How does time pass so fast? One minute I was celebrating with Nancy after her piano recital, and the next minute I was helping Darcy with her costume for the school play. (The truth is that a few days had passed, and it only *seemed* like minutes.) Unbelievably, my term paper was due in less than forty-eight hours, and I still didn't have a topic sentence.

"I want glitter, lots of glitter," Darcy said firmly. She was staring at herself in my bedroom mirror while I pinned up the hem on a billowy red cotton skirt.

"I don't think Snow White wore glitter," I told her for the fifth time. "After all, she wasn't a princess. She worked hard cooking and cleaning for the Seven Dwarfs."

Darcy sighed. "I thought this was supposed to be a fairy tale."

I grinned. Maybe Darcy had a point. "Okay, we'll spray a little glitter on the puff sleeves. That way the lights will pick it up, and you'll stand out on stage."

"Good. I want everyone to notice me." *Not a touch of stage fright*, I thought.

I spent the next couple of hours hemming her skirt and making a sash out of some leftover material. When the phone rang at nine o'clock, I was surprised at how late it was.

"Are you all finished?" Nancy asked.

"Not quite," I admitted. "I still need to put a drawstring in the blouse. The neckline is much too low."

There was a long pause. "I think one of us must be crazy," Nancy said finally. "I'm talking about your term paper."

"Oh, that!" I managed a little giggle. "I've got plenty of time to uh . . . polish it up." I hesitated. "I've been working on Darcy's costume for the play. The term paper is almost finished." *Definitely the biggest lie I had told so far.*

"Well don't put if off till the last minute," Nancy warned me. "Time has a way of creeping up on you. I'm still putting my footnotes together and it's taking ages. How about you?"

"I know what you mean," I said quickly. "Those footnotes can really get to you."

"And the typing!" Nancy went on. "I think I've used up a whole bottle of whiteout and I'm only halfway through."

I gave a sympathetic laugh. "Me too! I seem to make a mistake in every paragraph."

Nancy was all set to tell me a funny story about putting the carbon paper in the typewriter backward, when I decided enough was enough. If we talked about the term paper much longer, she'd know I was telling a giant fib. I told her I had to check some references, and quickly hung up.

I sat down at my desk and thumbed through my notes on the Civil War. I didn't even have a topic, and wondered what I could find that would be fast (and easy). Maybe I could write about one of the important battles, or one of the famous generals? Or maybe do something on the causes that led up to the war — Mr. Burrows would be bound to like something like that. The trouble is it was going to take time — a lot of time.

I glanced at the clock. Ten-fifteen. I had been sitting there longer than I realized and my term paper was due the day after tomorrow.

Time was running out.

You're probably wondering, Diary, if I worried about the term paper all the next day. I did my best not to, even though everyone talked about it all through lunch.

"I must have eye circles down to my chin," Candace muttered over her tuna salad. "Would you believe I was up till two this morning typing my paper?"

"At least you have a paper ready to type," Jessica said with a nervous laugh. "I'm only halfway through writing mine."

"You're both ahead of me," Samantha said, topping everyone as usual. "All I've got is a bunch of index cards and a rough draft." She waited for someone to say something, and Jessica and Candace moaned in sympathy, right on cue.

"Gosh, that's *awful*," Jessica said, shaking her head.

"What will you do?" Candace piped up.

Samantha tossed her long blonde hair over her shoulder and sighed dramatically. "I guess I'll just have to pull an all-nighter."

Later, Nancy shook her head disgustedly as we walked to English class. "Do you believe that?" she said. "The way Samantha talked, you'd think she hadn't done a single thing on her paper. What a phoney."

I nodded. "She probably just said that to get attention." All this talk about term papers was making me very uncomfortable, and I wanted to change the subject.

"By the way, are you finished with *your* paper yet?" she said, nudging my arm.

Darn! I knew she was going to ask me that.

"Um, just about," I hedged.

"Good, because I was afraid — " The bell rang just then, and both of us had to scurry to our seats before Mr. Rice closed the door. "I'll give you a call tonight," she whispered as we darted down the aisle.

Before I knew it, it was seven o'clock that evening, and the truth hit me. There was no way I had enough material for a term paper, even if I stayed up all night writing one! The only thing to do was make an emergency trip to the library.

I spent a frantic few minutes looking through the stacks, and came up with zilch! I decided it was time to talk to the reference librarian.

"The Civil War?" she asked wearily. "Usually we have a good selection of books, but as you can see, we're pretty much cleaned out right now." She shrugged. "Term paper time, you know."

"I know what you mean," I muttered.

She peered at me, and I think she knew exactly what was going on. "If only you had come in earlier, I would have been glad to help you," she said pointedly.

I swallowed hard. "Right. Well, thanks anyway . . ." Trying not to panic, I found myself heading for the mall. There was only one hope: Bookland.

The woman behind the counter yawned and glanced at her watch.

"I can order you some books on the Civil War," she said, checking a computer screen, "but they won't be here for a week or so."

"A week! No, I need them tonight. Immediately."

She motioned me vaguely toward the far wall. "Try aisle seven," she said. "Right next to the cookbooks."

"Impossible," I muttered, looking over the titles. There was nothing I could use, nothing at all. Now what?

Mom was in the kitchen, helping Darcy with her homework when I got home. It was nearly eight-thirty and time was running out.

"Nancy called," she said cheerfully. "She just wanted to tell you she's finished her term paper."

"Wonderful," I said, trying not to grit my teeth. What was I going to do!?

"Oh Lizzie," Darcy said, scraping back her chair. "I promised Tony you'd help him with his costume. He needs it for tomorrow."

"What are you talking about? Who's Tony?"

"He's one of the Seven Dwarfs."

"Darcy, there's no way I can make a costume for anybody tonight!" My mind was racing, and I felt like I was heading straight for a brick wall. The library was out, the bookstore was out. What was left — the encyclopedia?

"Puleeze, Lizzie," she said, tugging on my sleeve. "You won't have to make it. Just help me find Josh's old Santa Claus suit and he can use that."

"Darcy, I have no idea where it is."

"It's in the attic, but I can't lift the box down by myself. Puleeze!"

"Okay, okay." At the rate I was going, a few more minutes wouldn't really matter. "But if we can't find it right away, we'll have to forget it."

Darcy found the Santa suit in the first box she tried. With a yelp of joy, she pulled out the faded red jacket and pants. "Look, Lizzie, this will make a great dwarf costume, right!"

"Right," I said, my mind a million miles away.

And then I noticed a folder of yellowed papers in the bottom of the box. Josh's old school papers, I thought idly.

Probably nothing interesting, I decided while sifting through them. Old test papers, homework papers, and . . . even a term paper. A term paper!

It practically jumped out of the box at me. A term paper on the Civil War. It was impossible, but there it was. I must have gasped, because Darcy looked up in surprise.

"Are you okay, Lizzie?"

"I'm fine," I gulped. Actually, I wasn't fine at all. My pulse was zooming, and I felt faint.

The title looked impressive. "The Civil War: A Study of the Five Main Causes." Exactly the kind of thing a teacher would like. Exactly the kind of thing Mr. Burrows would like. Unless . . . he had already seen it? I frowned, trying to remember if Josh had been in Mr. Burrows's class. No, Mr. Burrows wasn't even teaching at Claremont when Josh went there.

If I wanted a term paper, I had one right in front of me. It was perfect, it was too good to be true.

I fingered the yellowing pages. Six pages, double-spaced. Just the right length. I could retype them, and — I stopped and shook my head. What was I thinking of? That was stealing. Outright stealing! I couldn't take Josh's paper and turn it in as my own. And yet . . . what choice did I have? If I didn't turn in a paper tomorrow, I'd get an F.

"Darcy," Mom yelled up the stairs. "It's nine-thirty. I want you to take your shower now."

"Okay, Mom," Darcy said, scampering ahead of me down the stairs.

I stood alone in the attic for a moment. Nine-thirty at night and the paper was due tomorrow. All I had to do was retype Josh's paper. The whole idea was scary. What if someone found out? I shut my eyes tight and tried to imagine what would happen. It would be *awful*.

"Lizzie!" Mom called. "I don't want you to stay up too late."

"Don't worry, Mom. I'll be right down." I hugged the paper to my chest and turned off the attic light.

I was about to do the scariest thing I had ever done in my whole life.

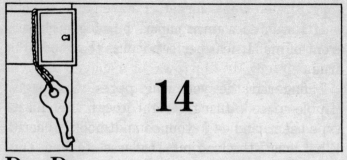

14

Dear **D**iary:

Once I made up my mind to go through with it, the rest was easy. It took me until two in the morning to retype Joshua's paper, but it was worth it. I read it over once more during breakfast, and couldn't believe my luck. The paper was good. Better than good, it was great. Joshua had done a lot of work on it, and I knew Mr. Burrows would like it.

If you're wondering, Diary, if there was a nagging voice inside me that said, "Don't do it!" you're right. I knew it was very wrong to take Joshua's paper, but I was out of time, and out of choices. I just had to take a chance!

Mr. Burrows was standing in the doorway when we filed in. "I want to collect your term papers right now, everybody, before we start class." He held up his hand to ward off a chorus of groans. "Please, no moaning, no excuses. You've known for weeks about the paper, so what's the big deal?"

He spotted me and shook his finger playfully under my nose. "I'm expecting great things from you, Lizzie. Don't forget, I haven't seen your rough draft, so your paper will be a big surprise."

A really big surprise, I thought. "You won't be disappointed, Mr. Burrows," I managed to say.

I headed for my seat, but stopped when I saw Mr. Burrows peering at my paper. "Say Lizzie . . . what happened to your computer?" He peered at me over his wire-rimmed glasses.

My heart thudded to a stop. "My computer?"

"I thought you said you used a word processor," he said, puzzled. "But this looks like it was typed." He held it up to the light and laughed. "I see you went through a lot of whiteout."

"I sure did. I . . . uh, ended up typing it after all."

"Computer on the blink again?"

"Something like that. You know how it is."

"That I do," he said feelingly.

I scooted to my seat without another word. My first close call, and I didn't like it at all! I felt nervous, guilty, and terribly worried. I knew I wouldn't be able to relax for a minute until that paper was graded and back in my hands.

Nancy and I celebrated that afternoon at the Zephyr.

"Wow! Aren't you glad that's over?" She tucked a napkin into the collar of her sweatshirt and attacked a Chocolate Zombie, one of the Zephyr's largest (and messiest) sundaes.

"I'm happier than you know," I told her.

"You know, for a while there," she went on, "I really wondered if you were ever going to get it done on time." She licked her spoon thoughtfully. "I'm glad I was wrong."

"I told you not to worry so much," I said lightly. *Now can we please change the subject!* "What are you going to do with all your free time now? Just think, you'll be able to spend some extra hours at the piano."

She knew I was teasing. "Yeah, right," she kidded me back. "Actually, I've got some good news. I'm not taking piano lessons anymore."

"You're quitting?" I couldn't believe it. "What about your parents?"

"We had this long heart-to-heart talk after the recital. I guess they finally realized that piano lessons were something *they* wanted, not something I wanted." She paused. "They said they were proud of me, though, and that they knew I had done my best."

"You really came through with that 'Mexican Hat Dance,'" I said proudly. "Not a single mistake."

She scooped up a giant blob of chocolate ice cream. "Isn't it funny how things work out? You were worried about your term paper, and I was worried about the piano recital. And both of us were just being silly because everything turned out great."

I felt a little chill go through me. My term paper hadn't turned out "great." Not yet, anyway. If Mr. Burrows ever suspected that I hadn't written it, my whole world would fall apart. Everything would come crashing down around me in a second! I wondered what Nancy would think of me if she knew the whole story.

"You know something?" Nancy said, gesturing with her spoon. "I've decided that from now on, I'm not going to worry anymore, because things really do turn out for the best." She raised her glass of ice water. "So here's to no more worry."

"Right," I said weakly, lifting my glass to touch hers. "No more worry." *No more worry?* I was terrified that my worries were just beginning.

I managed to relax for the next few days, mainly because Mr. Burrows didn't talk about our term papers very much. He said he had started to grade them, and left it at that.

You can imagine how surprised I was the following week, when he appeared with a giant folder tucked under his arm. "They're h-e-e-e-r-e," he said, sounding just like that little girl in *Poltergeist.*

"Our term papers?" Samantha asked. "How do they look?"

"Pretty much like I expected," Mr. Burrows said, drawing the moment out for all it was worth.

"And how's that?" Donald Harrington piped up.

For once, he forgot to act like a jerk, probably because he was worried about his grade.

"Some great, some not so great, and some" — Mr. Burrows sighed and shook his head — "rather disappointing. Let's get started, and I'll pass them out." He waited until we took our seats before opening the folder. The room was very quiet, and someone laughed nervously in the back row. "The moment of truth," he said.

I gulped. It seemed like he was looking right at me. *The moment of truth?* Could he possibly have discovered what I had done? A long moment passed as his eyes met mine. I almost forgot to breathe, and then he put on his glasses and began to thumb through the papers.

"However . . . I have one comment to make before I give these back to you."

I relaxed a little. Of course he had no idea that it was Joshua's paper. I crossed my legs and settled back in my chair, sure that I was out of danger.

"One paper is so completely different from the others, that I think I should talk about it a little."

I froze. He knew! He was looking right at me.

"I've read it three times," he said, "and I'm still not sure what to say to this particular student."

He had everyone's attention now, and I could see that Donald Harrington was leaning forward, trying to read the name on the cover sheet.

I didn't have to read the name. I recognized the double cover, the bright yellow construction paper, topped with a sheet of clear plastic.

It was my paper.

"I asked myself why did this student do what she did . . ."

"She?" Ericka Powell whispered from the seat next to me. "Who is it?"

I could feel my face getting hot. He knew, and in a few minutes, everyone else would know.

". . . and I finally decided that she was willing to go the extra mile."

Go the extra mile? What was he talking about? I slithered down in my seat, wishing I could make myself invisible.

Mr. Burrows walked down the aisle, straight toward me. "Yes, Lizzie," he said, smiling. "It's your paper I'm talking about."

I couldn't have said a word if my life depended on it, so I just stared at him.

"And I'm happy to say that it's one of the best papers I've ever read."

The best paper he ever read? Now I *really* felt guilty. Everybody was looking at me and I knew I had to say *something*. "It is?" I said weakly.

"You did a wonderful job, Lizzie. There's some good solid research here, and some very fine writing. I can see you put a lot of time and effort in it." He smiled and handed me the paper. "You've

101

got an A plus. The only one I gave in this class."

"Thanks," I said. My mouth was too dry to say anything else.

An A plus! You can't imagine how awful I felt, Diary. My plan had worked, but I felt like the world's biggest creep. I never expected to get an A on the paper. I thought maybe a C plus, or a B minus, tops. I had certainly fooled Mr. Burrows, but I felt worse than ever. I felt guilty. Incredibly guilty. I know my face must have been beet-red, and my stomach was in knots.

Nancy reached across the aisle and thumped me on the back. "Way to go!" she whispered happily. "I'm proud of you."

Great, I thought. If she knew the truth, she wouldn't be so proud of me. I felt like crawling in a hole.

I barely noticed that Samantha was scowling at me, and I tuned out the rest of the class. I couldn't wait for the bell to ring.

And then Mr. Burrows dropped another bombshell. I was walking out of class with Nancy, when he motioned me to his desk.

"Congratulations again, Lizzie. That's a fine paper."

"Thank you." I could hardly bear to look at him.

"In fact, it's so good that I'm passing it on to Mrs. Laurel."

"Mrs. Laurel?"

"She edits the literary magazine. I think a term paper like this deserves to appear in print."

Oh no! I was stunned. "You do?"

He nodded enthusiastically. "I've already given her a copy of it, and with any luck, she can fit it into the next issue. Just think, Lizzie. The whole school will get a chance to read your term paper. You're going to be a published author."

I felt like the room was swimming. Things had gone from bad to worse in a millisecond! If Joshua's paper ever turned up in a magazine, someone would be bound to remember it. I needed to do something quickly. But what?

"Lizzie, are you all right? You look a little pale."

"I'm fine," I blurted out. "I'm just surprised you think the paper is good enough to be published."

"I told you, Lizzie, I think it's excellent." He beamed at me through his wire glasses. "Your parents will be very proud of you."

Proud. There was that word again. Why would anyone be proud of the world's biggest phoney? I don't remember how I got out of the classroom, except I remember clutching Nancy's arm very tightly.

"Lizzie, are you sure you're okay? You really do look a little strange."

I hesitated. Nancy was my friend, the one person I could really trust. Did I dare tell her the terrible thing I had done? No, I needed to be alone to think things over. I was in the biggest mess of my whole life and I had no idea what to do next.

At seven o'clock that night, I was alone in my room, waiting for an answer to come to me. There *must* be some solution. But what? I flipped over my Empire State Building paperweight a few times and paced the floor.

It's funny how things pop into your head out of nowhere. I was glancing at my bookshelf, and I remembered a quote out of a Walter Scott poem we studied. "Oh, what a tangled web we weave, when first we practice to deceive." How true, I thought. I was in a tangled web all right. I felt just like a spider caught in a net. I had never in my wildest dreams thought things would turn out this way. It all had seemed so easy. Copy the paper, turn in the paper, get a grade. And then relax and forget the whole thing.

Except things had gone too well. Mr. Burrows not only liked the paper, he loved it! So much the worse for me.

A light tap at the door made me jump. Mom stuck her head in with a plate of something green and wiggly. "Ready for a snack?" she asked with a smile. "Microwaved zucchini skins. New from Roth's Frozen Foods." She grinned like someone doing a television commercial.

"Yuch!"

"I know," she added, plopping down on my bed.

"But what can I say? Your father says they're going to be hotter than cheese popcorn."

"I hate cheese popcorn." I paused and looked out the window, my mind a million miles away.

"Honey," Mom said softly, "you were awfully quiet during dinner. Is something wrong?"

I shrugged. How could I tell her the truth? I looked at her and my heart turned over. Part of me wanted to throw myself in her arms and confess everything. She'd know what to do, wouldn't she? But part of me felt so guilty and ashamed, I just couldn't bring myself to say anything.

"Lizzie, what is it?" She scooted off the bed and put her arm around my shoulder. "Something *is* bothering you, isn't it? I could tell at dinner."

I shook my head, and squeezed my eyes shut for a second. When I turned to face her, I was back in control. "Everything's fine, Mom," I said brightly.

"Really?" She looked at me very closely.

"Sure." I bobbed my head up and down. "The only thing wrong at dinner" — I managed a little giggle — "was that green bean casserole. Someone should tell Dad's boss that green beans and chili sauce don't mix. It was really yuchy."

"I know what you mean," she said, starting to laugh. "Except I've got news for you. That wasn't chili sauce." She paused dramatically.

"Don't tell me. It was — "

"You'll never guess. Not in a million years." She cracked up, and fell back on the bed.

"Tell me!"

When she spoke, her voice was muffled with laughter. "Grape jelly!"

"Grape jelly and green beans? Totally gross!"

In spite of the awful predicament I was in, Mom had managed to make me smile. She's really good at that. She stayed in my room for a few more minutes, and I actually nibbled a few of the zucchini skins.

When she left I felt really worried and depressed again, and the truth hit me. Nothing had changed. I was still in a terrible mess, and had nowhere to turn.

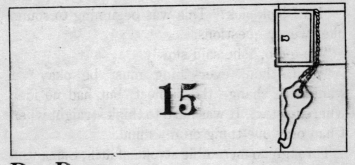

15

Dear **D**iary:

The next week passed very slowly. I felt like a big black cloud had settled over me, and I expected it to start raining on my head at any minute.

Nancy knew something was up, but had no idea what. "You sure are quiet," she said one day at lunch. "Is everything okay?"

"Why wouldn't it be okay?" I said, answering a question with a question, which is a really good way not to give an answer.

She shrugged. "I don't know. You just don't seem like yourself."

That was the understatement of the year.

"Then who do I seem like?" I teased.

She made a face. "Very funny." She picked at her wilted lettuce salad. They actually *call* it wilted lettuce on the cafeteria menu, which should clue you in to the fact that it's going to be wet and soggy. "You're not sick, or anything, are you?"

"Do I look sick?" This was beginning to sound like twenty questions.

"No-o-o-o," she said slowly.

"Well, then, everything must be okay." I wanted to change the subject, but had no idea where to start. It was hard to think straight when I had only one thing on my mind.

Through an incredible stroke of luck, Samantha and her friends decided to join us at that moment, and suddenly it was too noisy to make conversation. I know Nancy was still worried about me, though, because she kept staring at me every few minutes. I tried to smile reassuringly, as if I didn't have a care in the world. If she only knew, I thought. If she only knew . . .

By the end of the second week, I gave up. I just couldn't keep up the act any longer. I had to tell Nancy the truth. I needed some advice, and she was the one person I could always count on.

I caught up with her at her locker just as the dismissal bell rang. "Can you come over to my house right away?" I asked. "We need to talk."

"Sure," she said, looking a little surprised. "Is anything wrong?"

"I can't talk about it here."

I didn't say another word until we were safely in my room with the door closed, half an hour later. Mom had surprised us with a plate of oat bran brownies to take upstairs, and I offered one to Nancy.

"Hmm, not bad. Definitely one of the best things your Dad has come up with. Sure you don't want one?"

I shook my head. I was too edgy to sit still, and I paced back and forth over my braided rug.

"Honestly, Lizzie," Nancy said, through a mouthful of crumbs, "I wish you'd settle down somewhere. You're making me nervous. What's wrong?"

I plunked myself on the bed next to her. "Nancy," I said slowly. "I've made a terrible mistake."

She stopped eating immediately, her blue eyes serious. "What's up? What did you do?"

I didn't know where to start. "It's about my term paper . . ." I began. "The one for Mr. Burrows."

"You did a great job on it," she said, looking a little uncertain. "He was crazy over it."

"That's just it," I told her. "It's not mine."

"Of course it's yours. You turned it in, didn't you?"

"I turned it in, but I didn't write it." I took a deep breath. "It's an old paper of Joshua's. I found it in the attic and I retyped it with my name on it."

Nancy's hand flew to her mouth and the plate

of brownies overturned on my bedspread. "You what? You stole it? Oh Lizzie, how could you do a thing like that?"

"I don't know," I said miserably. "It was the night before the paper was due, and I was out of ideas." I felt so awful I couldn't even look at her. "I knew I had to have a paper by the next day, so I took Joshua's. I know now that it was a big mistake."

"It was a *terrible* mistake, " she said slowly. "The point is, what are you going to do about it?"

"That's what I wanted to talk to you about. If Mrs. Laurel publishes it, Joshua's teacher might see it and remember it. Or there's a chance that Joshua might even see it."

She nodded. "You can't let that happen," she said, standing up and scooping the brownies back onto the plate.

"What should I do? What would you do?" As soon as I asked the question, I realized how silly it was. Nancy would never find herself in a jam like this, because she would never steal someone else's paper. *Steal.* My stomach tightened at the word. I had stolen Joshua's paper, and felt so ashamed of myself.

"We're going back to school," Nancy said. She glanced at her watch. "If you hurry, you can still catch Mr. Burrows. The teachers never leave before four o'clock."

"Mr. Burrows?" I felt sick at the thought of facing him. "No! I just can't do it!"

"Lizzie," she said, looking puzzled. "You don't have a choice. You have to tell him what you did. It's your only way out of this mess."

"There's got to be another way," I said stubbornly.

"You're fooling yourself, do you know that?" As usual, Nancy was acting very reasonable.

"Maybe not," I insisted. "Maybe I can come up with something else."

"Lizzie, you're just not thinking straight." Nancy shook her head. "Believe me, you *have* to tell Mr. Burrows, and the sooner the better."

Nancy spent another half hour trying to persuade me, but I wasn't listening anymore. I was wrapped up in my own thoughts, still trying to find a magic answer. I wanted to get off the hook — without having to confess what I had done.

I found myself avoiding Nancy for the next ten days. Somehow seeing her just reminded me that I was in a terrible jam, and that nothing was settled. It wasn't anything she said, but Nancy has a way of getting her message across without saying a word.

I spent a lot of time thinking in my room. (Gram would probably call it moping, but then she had no idea what was really going on.)

111

I finally hinted to Gram that I had a big decision to make, but I didn't tell her what it was. We were sitting on her patio on a bright Sunday morning.

"Gram," I said slowly, "what would you do if you had something hanging over you all the time?"

"Hanging over you?" She paused, her blue eyes serious. "You mean like a cloud?" As usual she got right to the point.

"Or an axe," I muttered. She looked startled and I said quickly, "Oh, it's nothing that can't be fixed. I guess."

I must not have sounded too convincing because she moved her chair closer to me. "I'd try to shoo that cloud away," she said softly. "I'd do whatever it takes."

"That's just the problem. What if you don't know what to do?"

"I don't suppose you want to tell me exactly what the problem is?"

I looked at her and for a moment I was tempted. "Not yet."

"Well, it's hard to know what to tell you unless I know some specifics," she said. She folded her arms in her lap and looked out across the lawn. "But you know what, Lizzie?" She turned to face me and smiled. "Deep down, I think you know the right thing to do. I think you have the answer in your head right this minute."

112

I sighed. She was absolutely right. I leaned over and hugged her. "I love you, Gram. And thanks."

The moment of truth came the very next day. Nancy put her arm around me. "Just tell him exactly what you told me." She was trying to cheer me up, trying to be encouraging.

"It's going to be awful," I muttered, knowing that she was right. It was the only thing to do.

"It'll be pretty terrible," she admitted. "But I'll be with you every step of the way. You're going to get through this, Lizzie," she said, squeezing my shoulder. "You'll see."

"Promise?"

She nodded. "I promise. Now let's hurry."

The dismissal had rung half an hour earlier. Mr. Burrows was closing his briefcase, but stopped when he saw us.

"Hi girls. Did you forget something?"

I hesitated, and Nancy spoke up. "Not really," she said, nudging me forward. "I'll be out in the hall," she whispered.

"I have to talk to you," I said, sinking into a chair in the first row.

He must have known something was up, because he looked very solemn and took a seat next to me. "Okay, Lizzie. What's up?"

I licked my lips. "You know the term paper I turned in to you?"

"How could I forget it?" he said. He gave me a reassuring smile. "It was the best paper in the class."

I looked right into his eyes. "I didn't write it," I said softly. "Joshua, my brother, did."

He didn't say anything for a moment, and fiddled with his glasses. "Your brother wrote your term paper for you, Lizzie? Is that what you're telling me?"

"It's not like you think," I said quickly. "Joshua doesn't know I took his term paper. It's an old one I found in the attic." I paused. "In fact, he'd kill me if he knew I pulled a dumb stunt like passing it off as mine."

"A very dumb stunt," Mr. Burrows said heavily. His eyes looked very sad. Why wasn't he angry with me? I wondered. Anything would be better than seeing this disappointed look on his face.

"What's going to happen?" I said after a moment.

He shook his head. "I don't know, Lizzie. But I can tell you one thing, this is very serious. I'll have to tell the principal, and of course, your parents."

My parents! Mom was home right now, listening to the radio and fixing dinner. What would she do? What would she say?

"Why did you do it, Lizzie?" Mr. Burrows said, cutting into my thoughts.

"I don't know. I honestly don't." I stared at my hands. "I guess I just put off writing my own paper until it was so late . . ." I stopped, not sure what to say next.

"That it was too late?"

"Something like that."

"It's never too late, Lizzie," he said, standing up and walking back to his desk. "If you had come to me with your problem, I would have helped you, and even given you an extension. But this way . . ." He sat down and stared into space. He looked at the clock. "Let's get this over with right now, Lizzie. Mr. Thompson is still in his office, and your parents can meet us there."

The next ten minutes were terrible. Nancy and I waited together in Mr. Thompson's outer office while Mr. Burrows called my house.

"Your mother will be here in a few minutes," he said.

I nodded. I was afraid that if I tried to talk, I'd start crying, so I didn't say a word.

Mom rushed into the office at four-thirty. "Honey, how did this happen?" She hugged me very tightly.

"I don't know." Mom looked so upset, I started to cry. "I just ran out of time, and I knew I had to turn in something."

"She knows it was a mistake, Mrs. Miletti," Nancy piped up.

"That's very loyal of you, Nancy." Mom said

115

softly. "But I think you should run home now and let me handle this."

Nancy touched my arm. "See you tomorrow, Lizzie. It will be okay. Really."

"Where shall we start?" Mr. Thompson said when we all were seated in his office. He paused and stared hard at me. "I guess I'd like to ask you why you did it, Lizzie. It seems completely out of character."

I stared at my lap. What could I say? I knew that I had made the biggest mistake of my life. I glanced at Mom. She looked very worried, which made me feel worse than ever. In fact, everyone looked upset. I was surprised that no one seemed angry with me. Just very, very disappointed. I felt awful!

"I ran out of time," I said, and immediately lowered my eyes. What a crazy excuse, I thought. It was really no excuse at all. "Look, that's not the real reason," I said, looking Mr. Burrows right in the eyes. "I guess I just didn't want to do the term paper, so I put off doing it."

"You never thought of coming to me?" he said gently.

"Not really. I didn't know what I could say." I shrugged. "I had the same chance to do the paper as everyone else. The same amount of time . . ." I shook my head. "I really don't know why I let it go."

"I think I'd like to talk to your mother, Lizzie. Would you please wait outside for us?"

"Sure," I said unhappily. What were they going to say to Mom? Would I be suspended? What would Dad say!

Ten minutes later, they came out.

"We've come to a decision that seems fair to everyone, Lizzie," Mr. Thompson said.

"Okay," I said quietly. "What is it?" I noticed that Mom came and stood next to me.

"First of all, we've decided not to suspend you. What you did was very serious, and very wrong, but a suspension wouldn't accomplish anything."

"Thank you," I said in a very small voice.

"Naturally, you will have to do another term paper for Mr. Burrows. It's due in one month, and you won't receive full credit. Your grade will be lowered by two letter grades."

"So if you turn in an A paper, your grade will only be a C," Mr. Burrows explained.

"I understand."

"That's only fair to the other students," Mr. Thompson said. "The ones who turned in their papers on time." He looked at his watch. "It's getting late. I think the best thing to do right now is to go home, Lizzie. I want you to talk things over with your parents, and most of all, I want you to think about what you've done. Think about it very carefully."

"I will."

What else can I say, Diary? Mom was very quiet on the way home, and I stared out the window, wondering where to begin. How could I tell her how sorry I was? How could I begin to make it up to her? And how was I going to tell Dad!

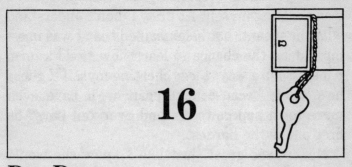

16

Dear **D**iary:

I don't know how to describe the past few days. I guess *terrible, awful, and embarrassing* would do for starters. But I think the worst is over now, and things are finally getting back to normal.

Dad took the news about the term paper better than I thought he would. I knew he was disappointed in me, but we had a long talk after dinner and I think we have everything straightened out. I know that I made a big mistake, and he knows that I know, and that it will never happen again.

That was probably the main thing that Mom and Dad wanted to talk to me about. Mom said that it's okay to put your mistakes in the past, as long as you know where you went wrong. (Do I ever!) And Dad added that he wanted me to promise to never even *think* about pulling something like that again. That was an easy promise to make. I felt so guilty and ashamed of myself, I know I'd never even be tempted.

Mr. Burrows reminded me that I wasn't only

119

cheating Joshua (by stealing his work) but that I was cheating myself. At first, I didn't understand what he meant, but he explained that I was missing out on the chance to learn how to do a term paper. So in a way, I *was* cheating myself. I guess he's right, because next year, we'll have even more term papers to do, and everyone says the first one is the hardest.

Nancy was great, just like I knew she would be. She called me the night we saw Mr. Burrows, and I told her what had happened. She listened without saying anything, and when I finished, I was surprised to hear her sniffling.

"Nancy, are you crying?" I asked, surprised.

"Oh Lizzie, I'm just so glad it's over." She stopped to blow her nose. "I've been so worried about you. I thought about you having to face Mr. Thompson and Mr. Burrows, and I just didn't know what would happen. I thought that maybe you'd be suspended." Then she said in a quavery voice, "I just don't know what I'd do if my best friend wasn't in school with me every day."

That made *me* feel like crying, and I started bawling right along with her! "Oh, me too," I sobbed. "I don't know what I'd do without you, Nancy."

After a couple of minutes of crying, Nancy started giggling "Hey, isn't this kind of silly?" she said. "I called to cheer you up, and look what happened."

I found myself laughing, too. "You're right, we shouldn't be crying at all. Things turned out better than I thought they would." I thought for a moment. "A lot better than I deserved."

Nancy tactfully didn't answer that one. "Well," she said finally, "at least it's over." I heard her yawning into the phone. "I guess it's time to turn in. Do you want to go to the Zephyr tomorrow after school? My treat."

"Nope," I said. "I'm meeting the reference librarian at three. And I'm tied up every day after school for the next month."

"Oh," she said, understanding at once. "Your paper."

"That's right. I'm going to turn in the best paper Mr. Burrows has ever seen on the Civil War." I laughed. "Well, I'm going to try to, anyway."

"You know what, Lizzie? I'm very proud of you."

"I'm glad. Have a hot fudge sundae at the Zephyr for me."

I hung up, feeling pretty good about things. I had made a mistake, but I had learned a lesson from it. I flipped open a book on the Civil War, and thumbed through a few pages. It's funny, but all of a sudden, I could think of lots of things to write about. Topics just jumped out at me, and I reached for my pen.

I tried a title. "A Look at Civil War Battlefields" by Lizzie Miletti. It sounded sort of interesting,

I thought. Yes, it was definitely a possibility. Or maybe "How the Civil War Was Won" by Lizzie Miletti. I liked that one, too.

I chewed on the end of my pen and stared out the window. It didn't matter which topic I decided on, because the important thing was the name on the paper. Lizzie Miletti. This time it was going to be for real. My name would deserve to be on the paper. I was going to do all the research and all the writing.

Good or bad, this term paper would be all mine. No more lies!